CHARMIE BHAYANI

AMALGAMATION OF ENCHANTING TALE OF
LOVE WITH SOULFUL POETRY

Live In A Dream

A JOURNEY OF UNFULFILLED DESIRES

BlueRose ONE.com
Stories Matter
NewDelhi • London

BLUEROSE PUBLISHERS
U.K.

For permissions requests or inquiries regarding this publication, please contact:

BLUEROSE PUBLISHERS
www.BlueRoseONE.com
info@bluerosepublishers.com
+4407342408967

ISBN: 978-93-7018-833-4

Cover design: Daksh
Typesetting: Tanya Raj Upadhyay

First Edition: March 2025

Dedicated to all college sweethearts
in India who seek their true love

ABOUT THE AUTHOR

Charmie Bhayani is a former Interior Designer turned full time mother turned author.

She has received her bachelor's in Interior Design education from CEPT University, Ahmedabad India in 2009. Raised in Oman, studied in India & Germany and now settled in Dubai, UAE, she has had the opportunity to see the world from a varied perspective.

Motherhood has encompassed her life extensively but that doesn't limit her love and passion for creativity and imagination to flourish.

Her love for writing had erupted during her University days itself. CEPT does have the potential to dig deep into your soul to bring out the best creativity embedded within you. Small poems were the best language of her expression. Her emotions were poured out mesmerizingly in forms of magical poetry.

However, she conceptualized and dived into the world of book writing in 2016 post her marriage. This book has been her passion and her baby ever since. She has finally been convinced to showcase it to passionate readers interested in romantic fiction and can't wait to see the response. Her aim is to touch the hearts of dreamy lovers of all age groups.

ACKNOWLEDGEMENTS

My writing, this story, is purely a magic of my mind. However, there are innumerable contributions of various people who enlightened me, supported me, encouraged me, had faith in my creativity, and/or were patient with me during my journey. Expressing my loving gratitude here to all those who have been holding my shaky hands and strengthened me with courage and words of wisdom.

- My biggest and strongest pillar is my husband (my Bau - *Hardik Bhayani*), who has believed in my talent and motivated me immensely every step of the way and never said no for anything. That's a rare quality in a husband.

- My parents- *Mukesh & Jaymala Kapashi,* from whom I learnt that happiness comes from being content.

- My professors, *Mr. Rajan Rawal and Dean Mrs. Krishna Shastri,* who appreciated my poetry writing, back in my University days, which strengthened my faith in my writing talent.

- My friend, *Ashit Gandhi*, who pushed me to set a deadline to publish this book.
- All my friends who have inspired me one way or another in shaping the characters of this tale of romance. Naming them would get awkward.
- My publishers- *BlueRose Publishers' team (Sameer, Meera, Sakshi, Akanksha, Dhruvi, Daksh & Tanya Raj).*
- My engaged, dreamy readers.
- Lastly, my son *Jivaan* for loving me crazily.

PREFACE

Life is simple.

But we complicate it with our unfulfilled desires. We tend to aspire for what we don't achieve, although it may not be meant for us. To most, it is being aspirational and ambitious, but to a few, it becomes dangerous and risky. Sometimes, our wishes end up affecting other's lives in a manner we could not have intended to or imagined.

Dreams are fantasies.

It is a sign of one being wishful and hopeful. But when our dreams complicate our lives and the lives of others, they become DREADFUL.

Destiny should be trusted.

We tend to believe that what we undergo is due to destiny. But when we aren't content with what we have, we curse destiny. Why can't we just trust our fate and believe that whatever we have is what we deserve and what is best for us?

Falling in love is beautiful.

But when the love turns into passion and then suppressed obsession, it becomes fatal. We don't realize what our emotional minds are capable of imagining. And how far can we be driven by our minds to achieve the unachieved? One must not allow suppressed emotions of love to dominate one's mind to an extent that they make your identity invisible.

Some love stories succeed to become marriages, and others become immortal. A few don't belong to either of the categories as they only ruin lives.

Here is one such narrative of a 'simple' romantic love story that turned into a 'complex' tragedy and ruined it all. The end will leave you jerked.

This story is a work of fiction but is inspired by true characters. As imaginative as it is, it will be relatable to each of you on some deep level, as it is eventually a reflection of on goings in our society.

LOVE......PASSION.....DESIRES...HEART BREAK.....FAILURE.....DISCONTENT MISERY

19 AUGUST 2016

PROLOGUE

THE MYSTERIOUS NIGHT

Clouds had extensively conquered the dark skies and decided to pour down heavily through this long night. Mysteries unimagined were to follow.

Saanvi, a middle-aged, pretty lady with a fair complexion, drenched in a light pink dress, having a mobile phone in her hands and a few hundred rupees crushed in her hand, rang the doorbell of a stand-alone villa in a residential community. A middle-aged man, Surya, tall, chiseled looking, with a husky complexion, a sharp jawline, and gym-trained body, dressed in shorts and a loose T-shirt, opened the door.

Saanvi looked at him, and tears rolled down her cheeks. She just bombarded him with agitation as she let herself in, uninvited, *"Oh my God, you are fine! Thank God! Why is your phone switched off then? Where have you been? Why are you ignoring me? Why weren't you there at the hospital with me, Surya? Have we had a fight? Where is Ashna? I have such a bad headache. I don't remember much."*

Surya, taken aback by this bizarre and extremely awkward encounter that had arisen, took a few steps backwards to comprehend what had just happened. He stared at her with curiosity and seemed completely nervous.

"Why are you staring at me as though I am a stranger? Is there something on my face? Were you busy, or are you angry with me? I know something is wrong otherwise, you would never do this. I was in the hospital for seven days and you didn't come to see me. Please tell me. You have never done anything like this ever since we got married."

Surya's eyes were almost popping out as he heard these rambling questions. He didn't have words to describe how amazed and startled he was. Putting himself together thoughtfully, he replied.

"You are shivering – here, take a towel. Wipe yourself. Relax, and please explain what's going on. I am super confused."

Another middle-aged pretty lady, Pooja, dressed in a long skirt and t-shirt with a 2-year-old kid in her arms, arrived from the bedroom and called out, *"Who is it, honey?"*

"Aaaaaaaaaa...........It's... it's...it's .....Saanvi." He replied with a shiver in his voice.

Saanvi pointed towards Pooja and asked Surya who she was.

Pooja judged Surya's dilemma and spontaneously took over by replying to Saanvi directly with a gesture to shake her hands, *"I am his wife, Pooja. Hi. We haven't met in all these years. But I have heard a lot about you. Glad to meet you finally."*

Saanvi froze still. She didn't understand what she had heard. Her head started wobbling on her neck, and her eyes began shutting. *"Surya, Surya"*, she called out as she dropped down. Her head bumped into the wall, and she fell down and lost consciousness.

Surya and Pooja were taken aback by what they had just witnessed. Little did they know that this mysterious night had come along with a whole baggage of unpredictable, life altering events to follow?

TABLE OF CONTENTS

JULY 2003

CHAPTER 1

RECAP – WHEN IT ALL BEGAN

Saanvi waited for the results of the Entrance Exams to be announced in a new town, Ajmer, far away from where she was brought up. Although she was a consistent topper back in School, a board rank holder, a talented performer, and a complete all-rounder, she had decided to pursue a career in the creative field of Design rather than something more academic like Engineering or Medicine.

Everyone knew she was different- full of life, always jumping around. She was studious but not geeky. She was a performer but not arty. She was a teacher's pet but not bitchy. She had a unique spark within her. She had a magnetic personality which we would call to have an X–factor.

Being a single child; her school friends and her parents were her world. Her School life had made her a confident, extrovert, motivated and an energetic individual.

But her emotional and sensitive side was known to all as well. She would get easily attached to anyone and pour her heart out to just anybody even loosely known to her. Her motto was to place trust in everyone. She would cry out loud even for the slightest little emotional scene of a movie. And hand out her every heartiest possession to a friend whom she cared for.

Her parents fulfilled all her desires at every stage of childhood. She was never refused anything she craved for. After all, she was the perfect child, always bringing pride to her parents in every aspect. Bringing back home awards, trophies, and certificates in everything she participated in was just a routine now. Achievements were an integral part of her life, which defined her competitive spirit at all times. However, thankfully, this quality did not transpire into arrogance.

Her humility was impeccable. She knew the value of what she achieved, but her roots were intact. She surely had no idea how she would react to a failure in life but yet she kept believing that she was simply lucky to win or succeed. Success did not distance her from her near ones. That's why she was loved by one and all around her. And she loved being adored by all. That was probably what drove her to strive for sincerity and perfection.

"Number six – Saanvi Rawal." Her name was announced. She had got admitted to the best Design University in the country. Stepping into the next phase of life was certainly filled with anxiety, but her self-confidence diminished her nervousness.

Living in the hostel without parents was not an option offered to her. Being extremely protective of her, her mother had decided to live with her during her entire University life of five years. Saanvi always felt deeply grateful as well as guilty for this huge sacrifice her parents were making for her. Little did she know that this wasn't a mere favor to her, but a solution to resolve their own fear? They feared that their daughter may get misled by peer pressure into wicked habits or wrong company.

Saanvi had built an image in her mind of college life. Bollywood movies played an important role in creating a perception about University life. Fun ragging, canteen sittings, bunking, hooting, singing, dancing, romance, friendships and last minute studying were what she desired her college life to be. And her desires were soon to come true. On her first day of college itself, she managed to have glimpses of all of these in her college.

She, along with a group of her batch mates, were forced to stay back for some ragging session by seniors. She was nervous but enjoyed it as well. Nothing was beyond tolerance. They were asked to dance and sing and do a naughty skit to entertain. It was a mean act played by seniors, but her sporting spirit to agree to seniors left them in splits. They were quite entertained by her humorous acts and impressed by her dancing skills. This made her instantly popular amongst the seniors. Now she was part of every ragging session and surprisingly her cool attitude added to the fun. One senior asked her to write a love letter to a senior girl and actually go find her and hand it over to her. The senior girl, on receiving the letter, was impressed with Saanvi's courage and gave her a peck on the cheek.

Her outspoken attitude and fearless response was enticing. She was given the responsibility to handle the fresher's party event to be held about three weeks after the college commenced. She had to organize all the performances by the freshers. This party was a tradition held every year to welcome the first-year batch and accept them as their own. Post the farewell party, there would be no ragging; the seniors and juniors would become friends as part of the tradition.

One of her batch mates, Rohan, had opted to play the guitar for his performance. He was a timid boy, always lost in his own world. She appreciated his talent, which boosted his confidence. He never spoke to anyone, but Saanvi was different. He began to like her. She, on the other hand, only saw her as a batch mate and never understood what feelings he had begun to develop.

College life became fun. It was a different kind of college. It remained open 24 hours for students to work on their projects. This environment, by default, provided a perfect platform for developing intimate friendships. All the first-year students became very tight friends. Ideating designs, sketching, late night tea sessions at the canteen, and loud music to energize the campus were permitted as well as encouraged by professors. After all, this was a design College, not a regular one. Saanvi had begun to enjoy this culture immensely. Hanging out with friends most of the time was her daily routine. Her mother was left with no choice but to accept these odd hours.

"All this freedom given to you comes along with a lot of responsibility on your shoulders. Don't ever misuse it, darling!" was a lecture she was reminded of almost daily. She knew her limits and never got influenced by a couple of hostelite batch mates to cross any lines setup by parents. She carefully chose her friends who were from the city itself, hence had parents around to protect them from any ill addictions or distractions.

Adulthood had begun, but not just yet. A couple of months later, on her birthday, her mother continued the tradition of celebrating her birthday with all her friends. All the batch mates were invited home. A well-planned act by the mother to review her new peers. Rohan also came down. All her friends got her little presents but Rohan didn't give her anything till the end. Later in the evening, her mother decided to leave the kids to hit adulthood alone for a while and left to go to a friend's house. This is when Rohan seeked the opportunity and requested Saanvi to sit in the center of the room. Saanvi, although embarrassed, couldn't dishearten him. She played along. Rohan took out five gifts from his bag and presented them to her one by one. All the other friends burst out in laughter and started mocking Rohan. Saanvi realized his romantic feelings for her. She, having no such feelings to reciprocate, decided to distance from Rohan gradually. She teamed with her friends and planned to fake a romantic affair with one of her batch mates, Surya, just so that Rohan would leave her alone eventually.

Surya had always sensed an embarrassed Saanvi when it came to Rohan. He didn't mind helping her out as a friend. During a group project, Saanvi teamed up with Surya so that Rohan would realize that she was getting distant. Rohan decided to mind his own business from then on.

This process of faking an intimacy didn't last long. It began to convert into something real and special. An unexplainable bond was flourishing. There was no mushy talk. It was pure friendship. They enjoyed teaming up and found immense comfort in each other. They had entered the friend zone too deeply to let them realize what they had begun to feel about each other.

Coincidently, Rohan had to leave the city as his father got transferred in a few weeks. However, this didn't end the intimacy of Surya and Saanvi. They shifted seats in the class and began to sit next to each other. Friends began to tease them, but strangely this didn't bother them at all.

"We are best buddies, guys. Nothing more. You all know that!" Saanvi would staunchly answer back to all the jokes made at them. But Surya never reciprocated. The seed of love had emerged in his heart, and at a subconscious, deep level, he had already started wishing for all the rumors to turn out to be true.

Surya Rana, a single child, was born and raised in Ajmer and got easily attached to Saanvi. A handsome, fair-skinned, tall, lean guy with a smart haircut could be a perfect description for his appearance. His humor was his skill to attract friends, and his caring nature was what attracted Saanvi towards him. His exposure to the world may not have been as much as Saanvi's, but his wit was magnetic.

Single children have a tendency to search for warmth in friends. Having no siblings tends to create a deep void in their adolescent years. This usually gets filled up only through friends. Surya and Saanvi had a similar void. They were filling it for each other. They understood each other. They would finish each other's sentences. Their ideas would match in any teamwork.

The semester was coming to an end, which was the timing for a College Christmas party. Saanvi and

Surya had, as usual, jointly taken responsibility for arranging to buy the snacks. They took off on his bike. It was almost 8 pm and dark. Adding to the already existing romantic setting, the street lights weren't on that evening for some strange reason.

The dark streets gave him courage or built up a mood, and he made up his mind. *"Saanvi, come closer – have to tell you something."*

She moved closer to him on the rear seat of the bike and grabbed his shirt tight, *"ya, what happened?"*

The stretch on his shirt got him sweating in the chilly winter. The cool breeze brought a shiver in his already trembling voice. With an amalgamation of low confidence and anxiety, he whispered, *"I love you!"*

Her ears heard the words, but her mind wasn't ready to process this known but new information. There was a level deep down in her subconscious which saw this coming, but her alert, practical mind had convinced her not to become prey to this upcoming brewing romance. She chose to stay silent.

"I said, I love you." He repeated, this time a bit louder.

"I know. I heard. I just don't know what to say. You are my best friend. This love angle just spoils friendships. Please let it not get in the way of our amazing friendship. I have never gotten close to a guy like this. We have such a great bond. Why ruin it?"

"Ok." His disappointment was clear in his voice. He knew she loved her too. But her lack of courage and state of denial was evident.

He didn't say anything else, and neither did she, for the entire bike journey. They returned to the College for the party and remained distant from each other. Surya left the campus without saying goodbye to Saanvi. She followed him to the parking area and stopped near his bike.

"See, see – now you see what I was worried about. Look how this love thing ruined our friendship. I told you. You are punishing me now. That isn't fair. It's not that I don't like you. You know it. It's just..."

"It's just what?"

"My parents are really strict. You are from UP, and I am from Gujarat. They are very conservative. They don't believe in inter caste/state love marriages. Forget the intercaste stuff, they won't accept love marriages. And they will never accept this relationship. I don't want to start anything which I know has no future."

"Don't you think you are thinking too deep into this? We are in our first year of college. And I said I love you. And I just expect you to say it back if you do too, and I know you do. I can sense it. I am not blind. That's it." Surya expressed his feelings with clarity and honest.

"I don't know."

"It's ok. I can't force you. I said what I felt. Bye."

He left Saanvi thinking and fighting with her emotions. She didn't have an answer for him. She knew he was right. But she didn't know how to say it back. She had promised her mother that she would never cross the line. To her, being in a loving relationship with Surya meant betrayal to her mother. But her inner voice knew that not saying 'I love you' back to Surya meant betrayal to her own heart and to his. She had romantic feelings for Surya. She had only pretended to live in denial. Her bond with Surya was evidently beyond friendship.

The next day was a long, stretched, painful day at college. There was no interaction with each other. Surya was disappointed in Saanvi for not being honest about her feelings. In fact, Surya didn't talk to anyone that day. His silence was killing Saanvi from within. She knew she was responsible for his melancholy. Her behavior had taken away his sparkling smile that used to be the reason she was cheered up all day.

Towards the end of the day, as Surya made his way out of the classroom, Saanvi held his wrist firmly and stopped him.

"I love you too. Please don't avoid me. I can't lose you." Her heart raced faster than the second hand on a clock.

"What? Are you serious?" He was more shocked than pleased. His disbelief was obvious, knowing how serious she sounded just a day before this.

"Yes. I love you." she accepted.

She hugged him cozily. He pressed his hands around her, with one hand on her head. He behaved like a caring parent more than a lover at that moment. He didn't want her to make any decision under any pressure - he realized.

"Let's go someplace else. It's time we have a talk."

They pushed off to a coffee shop, which technically transformed into their first date. They looked into each other's eyes. *"I can't believe I am doing this. I had planned that I would not get into this love business and be a perfect girl to my parents. Focus on my studies. But I can't lose you. You mean a lot to me. And like you said, let's go with the flow. We have an unsaid connection. I have never felt this before."*

"Well, for me, it is the first time I have ever felt like this for anyone. More than you, it is what we share that is invaluable. It is magical. I feel special with you. And I want to make you feel special all the time. I want to be there for you. And I know you are there for me." Surya expressed.

They walked out holding hands. It was special - the moment, the feeling, the bond, the space. They moved towards Surya's bike, which was parked near a dark spot. They got a chance to hug each other. They looked into each other's eyes, and gradually, their lips leaned towards each other. Their first kiss happened. Saanvi had a tear in one eye and tingle in both. Surya moved away and kissed her forehead. *"It is love, pure love. I will take care of you."* He assured her.

She came back home with guilt in herself. She had broken her promise to her mother. But her heart and mind were divided by two extreme emotions, and she had chosen to follow her heart. She didn't tell her mother anything about Surya and decided to keep it that way till she could.

'Surya and Saanvi' were an item now, the official first and only couple of their batch. Nobody was surprised with this news. Hence, now no one had to tease them, as they had announced their relationship openly to all their friends. Movie, puppy and mushy love was in the air.

MARCH 2007

CHAPTER 2

MAGICAL TIME

It had been over three years of smooth dating and academia. Surya and Saanvi were madly in love with each other. Their passionate love for each other was known to professors as well. They would always give a little peck of a kiss to each other for small little things. They would hang around together all the time. Every little workshop they did was together. Any group project for any course was taken up together.

However, their closeness did not distract them in their performance at College. They always used their talent and skills to enhance each other's work. They would not fail to help each other and tip each other to improve. They were both career oriented and passionate to excel in their work life. Both of them always scored well and were consistent rank holders in the class. They were the source of growth for each other. Their love was their strength.

One evening, they were hanging out at the coffee shop after classes, and Surya abruptly asked Saanvi, *"Do you trust me?"*

"Obviously. What a silly question! We have been together for three years. Why suddenly this random question?" she replied with complete conviction.

"Then why is it that you push me away whenever I try to come close to you? I mean, you just don't want to get intimate. Why?"

"Well! You know I am a bit conservative. This all has to happen after marriage. I am an Indian girl and believe it or not, a bit old school."

"You really live in the 60s. That is so outdated. Don't you ever fantasize about sleeping with me?"

"NO. Why do you?"

"Obviously, yes; almost every day, ever since we started dating. I am shocked you don't. It means you don't love me enough."

"That is such an unfair conclusion. But I am not going to defend myself as I don't think I need to prove anything."

"Ok, fine. Don't get so touchy. Just asked. You know I won't do anything without your consent and happiness."

"Well, thank you. Can we change the topic now?"

Getting intimate was the only thing missing in their perfect relationship. However, that never affected their mushy love.

A couple of weeks later, the Dean announced an adventure, *"Dear students, after months of efforts and planning, our college has finally got an opportunity to take the best students on a College trip. We will be sending our 'fourth year' top students for a learning experience to Italy to learn architecture and make amazing sketches and research for one whole month. This is a huge opportunity for you guys. Getting to travel to another country on University expenses and getting introduced to a new spectrum of learning. So buck up and work your butts off. As whoever excels will get this opportunity. Best of luck."*

The entire class worked hard throughout the semester. Exams were over, and the results were out. They weren't unpredictable. Saanvi was at rank 1, and Surya was in the 4th position. The first four rank holders were getting this opportunity to go. Everyone was thrilled except for Saanvi.

"Aren't you happy we are getting such a huge opportunity? You seem lost." Ananya, her friend, who was also the third rank holder, asked Saanvi.

"No, dear. I am thrilled that we are getting this opportunity, but I am upset as my mother has already refused to send me. She's too protective about me," disheartened Saanvi reverted.

"Why would she say no? People crave something like this. I think you should inform the Dean," she advised, and Saanvi was convinced to do so.

The Dean was very supportive and asked Saanvi to send her mom to her for a word. The Dean explained to Saanvi's mother, *"Sarita Ji, you cannot be so protective with your child. I am a mother too. Both my daughters have been in the States studying for the last five years. Students beg for an opportunity like this. And your daughter has achieved it on a silver platter after working hard. You cannot be an obstacle in her growth due to your fears and inhibitions. Set her free. Let her be. Additionally, it's a matter of just a month."*

Sarita Ji's outlook was given a new direction. She gained slight confidence in sending her child away from her. She decided to give it a thought.

She discussed it with Saanvi's Dad, and finally, after a few weeks of perusal by friends and family, she was convinced, but her fears hadn't disappeared. An Indian mother somehow feels responsible for their daughter until they get married off. It is the norm.

So, Saanvi, Surya, Ananya and Karan (the four rank holders) set out on a journey to a new destination by September, filled with lots of mixed emotions. They were all close friends already so it was going to be a complete rocking time.

However, it was going to be a whole new angle in the love life of Surya and Saanvi. Not only was this going to be an amazing learning opportunity for them, but their love was also going to blossom beyond limits. Close proximity brings along deeper attachments.

Saanvi, being away from her mother's daily stay in limits' pressure, allowed her inner self to emerge. She drew a lot closer to Surya. They were together 24 x 7 now. They would spend most of the time in each other's rooms, cuddling on the bed.

Winters in Europe were an added catalyst to their romance. Temperatures were dropping as days passed. It was freezing, and they hugged tight to feel the warmth of each other for more than just a few minutes.

"I know you are never going to be ready to take this to the next level. But for me, it's no longer a matter of any concern. I don't care. Our love is pure. And what we have is too special. Our hearts are one. Our souls are united. We are inseparable." Surya whispered his heart out. It was magical.

Saanvi felt so secure in his arms. She knew he was the one for her. He would never expect anything from her that would discomfort her. He would never push her for anything unreasonable. She had found her soulmate. *"I am married to you in my mind already. You are my world."*

Her world was complete now. She visualized her entire life with him in this one exhilarating moment. They remained in each other's arms throughout the romantic night.

Surya (*the sun*) and **Saanvi** (*the dusk*) were the two halves of a unit that would complete to become one whole.

They were meant together. These were the emotions running through her mind while cuddling up against the love of her life. She could stay like this for an eternity. But certainly, that was possible only in movies and television series. Movies never showed the scenes after that beautiful long cuddle. There would be a "The

End" after that "Special Hug". But this was not a movie. This was real. There was a life awaiting them with a lot of twists and turns after this Magical moment.

RULES

In my own set of rules
trapped and jailed
spontaneity and fun
is where I failed.

In the process
of making no mistake
I led a life;
that was nothing but fake.

Unnaturally dependent,
on my decision
every experience
was reduced to a mere mission.

Arriving here
has made me realize
that natural response
could be tried.

As it did no harm
instead, I made my self-built pressure
a little more calm.

Now, I wonder if breaking all rules
jumping into the game
which has no order,
no restriction, no name.

Guided by feelings and emotions,
would that solve all my desires?

JANUARY 2008

CHAPTER 3

TRUTH UNFOLDS

It had been two months since they had gotten back from their 'fantasy land' learning spree. Saanvi had gone back to her hometown for the summer holidays. Surya was in Ajmer enjoying his holidays. They were not going to see each other for the next three months.

Saanvi's emotions had peaked for Surya to the maximum. Her restlessness was evident. It had become extremely difficult for her to hide her emotions from her parents, and now she didn't want to. She knew she had entered into the zone of clarity where she wanted to stop playing hide and seek and open all her cards. But it wasn't easy for her. She had never disappointed her parents in any way. What if telling them about Surya would make her a less perfect child?

She battled her emotions and did not still have the courage to state facts.

But as they say, when you wish for something, it turns into reality without any direct effort by you. Sarita Ji happened to come across a chat exchange file between Surya and Saanvi on the desktop screen.

It wasn't rocket science to figure out what was budding between both of them. Their perfect child had crossed the line and fallen into a romantic affair with a boy of another caste. This was unacceptable and a matter of shame to their family. This was her perspective. Saanvi's emotions and love were irrelevant. Surya's heart of gold was immaterial. He is defined by his caste and not by his deeds or behavior in Sarita Ji's eyes. A nice boy who could win her daughter's heart by his unimaginable love was all mediocre in comparison to the fact that he did not belong to the same caste as them.

"Isn't Surya that thin, tall guy who came home once along with your friends? This is what all these good looking boys do. Trap girls into their love. He was with you in Italy as well, right? Oh my God, Saanvi! What have you done? I knew it. That's why I feared to send you alone away from me. Going alone with boys, obviously; at this age; you didn't remember your values? Does anyone know? What will society say? This is so embarrassing. He is of a different caste also.

This is not a match. Our family doesn't approve. They don't know our rituals and values. No one from our family gets married outside our caste. They have a different belief system, and their approach in everything is extremely different from ours." Sarita Ji kept mumbling for hours without letting Saanvi respond.

Her father came home to see Sarita Ji weeping loudly. *"See what your daughter has done? Read this. To whom will I show my face? I can't live anymore. I raised you with so much perfection. We made so many sacrifices. You didn't have the courtesy to respect any of it. I am shattered...."* She kept mumbling with tears.

Saanvi's father was also at a loss of words and shocked. *"Why, dear? Didn't we give you enough love; that you needed to go out to find more love? I think we must have done something bad in some life that we have to pay for our sins, Sarita. Otherwise, Saanvi was a lovely girl. She would have never done something so ridiculous."* He started weeping too.

Saanvi knew her parents would be disappointed. But she sure hadn't expected this kind of extreme response. She saw tears in her father's eyes for the first time. This shook her. She couldn't believe. She had turned from a perfect child, the apple of their eyes, into the child whom they were ashamed of now. Just for loving a nice, kind, and loving person, she had to pay such a big price. She didn't have words to defend her love. She didn't have courage to stand for her heart. She knew she had done nothing wrong, but her parents' harsh words were like spears into her heart. She kept silent for three days. She didn't talk to her parents and didn't go out of the house.

"That's it. I can't take it anymore. You tell Surya right away that it is all over. You have to end things with him; else I will end my life. I am suffering. Can't you see? Don't you have any pity for your mother? I was waiting for you to tell me that you would end it with him but it was my mistake to expect any sense from you." Sarita Ji fired Saanvi. Her mother's threat crushed her. Her pain was written all over her face. But she wasn't a rebel. She couldn't stand up for her wishes. She picked up the phone and dialed Surya's number. Her left eye rolled a tear with every passing ringtone. Those few seconds felt like a million years. Surya picked up the phone.

"My parents found out. As expected, they didn't approve. It's over. I am so sorry. Don't call me back, please." Saanvi couldn't express her pain. She was so shattered; she couldn't feel her pain anymore.

"Happy Ma?" she taunted her mother and locked herself in the room.

"You don't realize it now. But what I have asked from you is for your good future life. He wasn't right for you. He isn't of our caste. It's not a match. Our family would never accept this. You will thank me later." Sarita Ji defended her ideology while screaming.

Surya didn't call back. He knew something had gone very wrong. He didn't know how to react to this. He asked Ananya to call Saanvi and find out what had happened.

Ananya called her and inquired what had happened. *"Saanvi, you have to tell your parents how much you are in love with Surya. I am sure they will understand. It will take time, but they have to."* Saanvi, in her melancholy voice, replied, *"I can't convince them. They are not chilled out like your parents. My parents are very conservative. Please give Surya a message from my side. I love him a lot. But I don't have the guts. I will have to end this here. I am betraying him, I know, but I have to choose from one of my eyes."*

THE ONLY GAIN

Glaring eyes stared at me
with immense curiosity
waiting impatiently
for one of my eye
how could I?

When I knew I'd remain
with only loss and pain.
The eye I'd give
would have sorrow
and the one I'd keep
would have a tear of joy.

But either way, I'd remain
with only loss and pain.

Why was I chosen
to make such a choice
when neither my heart's right
nor my mind's voice?

'Coz with the choice I'd remain
with only to choose loss and pain.

And then, with trembling eyes
I made a firm decision
*to choose the so-called '**right**' one*
with extreme dissatisfaction.

Today, yet again
I remain
with THE ONLY GAIN
MERE PAIN.

Saanvi lay on the bed, staring at the ceiling. She didn't speak a word the entire three months. She didn't meet anyone. She had forgotten what it was to smile. Her eyes would be filled with sadness, and they would be watery almost all day. She had become a living dead body.

The holidays were over, and she had to get back to college for her final semester. She was asked to promise that she would not talk to Surya, even in college.

She reached the campus and looked at Surya. They stared at each other from a distance. They slowly walked towards each other. She had tears in her eyes. She hugged him tight and whispered in his ears, *"I can't betray my mother, so I have to betray you. Just hug me for the last time so tight. I want to live my entire life in this moment. I am just going to be soulless without you my entire life. "*

Surya didn't say anything back. He swallowed all his sadness and hugged her tight for a few minutes. They moved away from each other, and he kissed her forehead.

It was a goodbye kiss forever.

They didn't talk to each other alone ever again. They would only be together in the presence of friends and still never look eye to eye. The semester passed by, and they focused more on their academics. It was the day of convocation and the last day they would be seeing each other ever. The tension between them was too stressful. But Surya had decided not to put Saanvi in a tight spot. He had convinced his heart with immense difficulty that he had to let Saanvi choose what her priority was. And if he wasn't her priority, he couldn't force himself on her.

Saanvi walked up to Surya and asked him to meet her at the rear of the canteen alone. Surya, without any extra thought, reached there.

She held his hand and told him, *"We are soulmates. We may not be able to live together, but you will remain in my heart till I die. I know that the last word that I will say on my deathbed will be your name, Surya. That is what you mean to me. I know you will hate me for what decision I am taking, but that will never stop me from loving you. Goodbye."*

She kissed him for the last time. It was a long kiss, but this time, it was not a romantic one; instead, it was a tragic one. Both of them had tears rolling down their cheeks while kissing each other.

A beautiful, sweet, and romantic love story ended.

SOLITAIRE

What is that noise?
It creeps me.
Is it a bird on a tree
or raindrops falling into the sea?

It all seems
to build up my curiosity
forcing my dying thoughts
to unsolve the mystery.

But as my eyes open
into the world of reality
and my visions and imaginations
are driven far away from me.

I realize
the sound I hear
is of ***Silence***
and solitaire it leaves me.

Saanvi moved back to her hometown for good. Surya, Ananya, Karan, and a few other friends remained a gang back in Ajmer. Saanvi didn't keep in touch with anyone. All of them moved on to building their respective careers but used to hang out every once in a while. Ananya tried keeping in touch with Saanvi. But it was only small talk and usually a one-sided conversation. Eventually, she too got busy and gave up on this futile effort and stopped calling Saanvi.

NOVEMBER 2009

CHAPTER 4

BETRAYAL

Out of the blue, Ananya received a call from Saanvi almost a year later.

"Hi! I am getting married." Saanvi said in a low voice.

Ananya wasn't sure if Saanvi was excited to share this news with her.

"That's great. Congratulations. Who is the guy?" She replied with little excitement, as though trying to cheer Saanvi up.

"His name is Ambar. He is a nice guy. I have met him once and spoken to him a couple of times on the phone. I said ok. The wedding is in December. You and everyone else are cordially invited. I will really feel nice if you come. Shall send you the official invitations by post," Saanvi explained with minimum enthusiasm.

"Ya sure. We will come, but how come so suddenly? I mean, give me some details. When did you start seeing guys for marriage?"

"Right after returning from Ajmer. My parents thought that before I ran away with Surya, they should find me a groom. I kept rejecting guys for a year and requested them to stop showing me guys any further. But they just didn't stop. I had seen almost thirty-plus guys when I gave up. So, I decided to pick the most tolerable from all the guys I had seen so far. I chatted with Ambar and checked if it was okay to take it forward in spite of all the rejections earlier. He said he was fine. He seemed caring and happened to like me, so I decided to go ahead. My parents are happy and relieved. So, I am going along."

"Are you sure you can live with someone whom you don't love?"

"I will learn to love. It's an arranged marriage. This is how arranged marriages work, right? Also, do I really have a choice? If I don't say yes now, I will continue being pushed into the circus of looking for more eligible bachelors of my caste in town. I am ok."

"Well, if you have made up your mind. Give your heart and soul to your marriage. I know your situation and don't want to comment on anything otherwise. Just one quick question. Should I tell Surya about it?"

"Yes! Please do!" Saanvi replied gulping a lump in her throat.

Ananya brought it up when they all were gathered the next weekend. *"Guys, so I got a call from Saanvi on Tuesday. She is getting married. She has invited all of us."*

Nobody replied for a couple of minutes. All of them looked at Surya as though for approval. He was startled, but trying to hide his true sentiments. He said, *"It's ok. You guys should go. She is a friend."*

"She has invited you too." Ananya clarified.

"Well, I can't go. I have work." He tried to stall the real answer.

"Come, Surya. You have to get over it. Or talk to her, try to bring her back."

"I think we have been through this conversation, Ananya. I don't want to bring her back. I love her, so I'll let her go. If I were obsessed about her, I'd try to bring her back. She has made a decision, and I will have to respect her decision no matter what. It's just that I can't see her. It's going to bring back all the memories. I am trying too hard to forget her. You guys have helped me a lot. Seeing her getting married to someone else is going to kill me from within. I can't die once again. Please don't bring this up ever." He

finally opened up, and drops of tears filled the corner of his eye.

It was like he wanted to cry out, howl at the top of his voice, but the little tear just swallowed all his sorrows. 'It was over', he thought to himself. 'She is never coming back; his last small hope also was officially murdered. She was moving on, a bit too fast.

Ananya walked up to Surya and tried to console him. *"She didn't sound excited at all. She is just making a compromise."*

"Why? Why is she doing so if she isn't even happy? Can't her parents understand this much?" Anyway, I don't care. I just need to learn to get out of these thoughts." Surya handled the whole scenario with the utmost maturity. Behaving like a true gentleman, he didn't make a scene. He didn't try calling Saanvi to remind her of their love. He felt if she was moving on, that was what destiny had in store for them.

But Saanvi called Surya after a few days to invite him as well. *"Please come. Let's try to remain friends forever,"* she requested him.

"It's not possible to remain friends with you, Saanvi. Don't expect that. Please, I request you. You are moving on. I am happy for you. But I can't see you with

someone else. So, I can't come. Congrats and best wishes," he replied.

His reply was like a dagger in her heart. She knew she had done too wrong. Letting him go away from her life without any effort was the biggest guilt she had to carry in her heart all through her life. Everyone saw her moving on, but no one saw her inner pain. She didn't let anyone know of it. She was going to pretend to be happy as she didn't want to upset her parents ever again. She had to please everyone. It was her inner personality. She couldn't be imperfect. So, she was going to pretend to be a happily married girl and please her husband in the best manner possible. That's the decision she had taken for herself.

FAKE LIFE

A few steps ahead
I thought I had made
where did I know
I was in the wrong flow.

Instead of the shore
I had reached the core
from where all I saw
was my own reflection.

Now, fear builds up high
on memories merely can I rely?
Once again, my faith has gone
and I ask, will there ever be dawn?

Destiny brutally
refuses to reply.
Leaving me hopeless,
disheartened, and sigh.

Now I know for sure,
my desires and vision for happiness
are merely a dream
which I am forced to suppress.

Crushing my last hope
I decide to lead a fake life,
with no emotions, no desires,
and no time to revise.

Ananya, Karan, and all their other friends visited Saanvi's hometown for her wedding in December. Saanvi introduced them to her fiancé, Ambar, who was tall, good-looking, with a symmetrical physique an a fair complexion. He had a smile to die for, with a little dimple on his left cheek. He was a couple of years older than Saanvi. A good-looking geek was the perfect way to describe this handsome hunk. But his main qualification was that he was the same caste as Saanvi. He was working in an MNC in Paris. He had a very different career background from Saanvi's, so compatibility was yet to be discovered. But together, they did make a good-looking pair.

Saanvi was dressed in a red and white sari and donned in glittery gold jewelry in her dressing room. She looked like a princess. Karan came up to her and hugged her. *"You look like an angel"*, he complimented. She smiled back. They all knew what she was truly feeling. They gathered around her. *"So, tell us the story about Ambar. How did it all happen? How is he?"* Ananya enquired.

"He is a great guy; very loving and caring. I have met him only once at a coffee house and then spoken to him over the phone. He lives in Paris, so we didn't meet the second time until a few days ago when he got back from Paris for the wedding preparations. But we have been

so busy shopping and planning that we haven't really had the chance to be alone since. Don't know the real him yet. It's a lifetime of exploration here on," she explained.

"How did he react to the whole Surya issue?" Ananya checked hesitatingly.

"Well, it wasn't an issue, as I didn't tell him anything. I don't want to complicate things."

They were all quite amazed after hearing this. But it wasn't the right place nor the right time to discuss this topic further. It was her life, and she had the right to live it on her terms. They gracefully went ahead and enjoyed the celebrations.

Saanvi had made peace with her life. Her new life in Paris with Ambar was going to be something she would work on. She had decided not to look back into the past ever. Ambar was her future, and she had to give it one hundred percent. She had zero expectations in return from Ambar. They were new to each other and had to start from scratch. There was an initial awkwardness. However, that's what honeymoons are for. The one week they got to spend with each other in Switzerland immediately after the wedding shed away all discomfort.

Much to Saanvi's surprise, Ambar turned out to be a perfect husband. He respected Saanvi and her career. He loved her wholeheartedly and gradually became a 'hard-to-find' green flag husband. He gave her all the freedom and expected nothing back. Saanvi became very comfortable with Ambar.

There was no reason for her to feel any void. Yet, there was something within her that didn't allow her to be completely happy. At times, she would suddenly wake up from her sleep and rush to the washroom, locking herself up and crying. This happened to her often. Ambar would ask her what was wrong. She would just avoid answering by saying that she missed home and her parents.

She couldn't stop herself, and one day after a few months, she messaged Surya on Facebook.

"Hi. I know it's abrupt. But please keep in touch as friends. I am very happily married, but I don't want to stop being in touch with you. I request you."

"I am not sure. I will try," he replied after a few days.

They continued to remain cordial on chat, on and off. Her midnight awakenings reduced and gradually disappeared. They had probably been signs of guilt that she experienced for Surya.

Keeping in touch with him lessened the guilt. She had moved on, but a tiny part of her brain had kept Surya stored in her memory, and that didn't allow her to completely disconnect from his thoughts.

Saanvi couldn't focus on work or home wholeheartedly. She worked but only to kill time. There was nothing that was dissatisfying in her life, but she was unable to live it to the fullest.

On the other hand, Surya concentrated all his energies on his career. He worked so hard day and night and started achieving great heights. His projects made a name for him in the field of design. He had articles published in design magazines about his projects.

JULY 2013

CHAPTER 5

REAL SPLIT UP

Four years flew by. Saanvi and Surya had become friends again by now. They would share any new events happening in their lives through social networking sites and text chat. They would chat once in a week or 10 days.

Saanvi had become a lot more focused on her career. She was far more committed to Ambar than before. All her melancholy and pretense had gradually begun to vanish. She had genuinely started experiencing happiness. Surya's friendship was enough for her to keep her in place.

"Hi Saanvi, I thought of messaging you so that you don't find out from someone else. I am getting engaged. Her name is Pooja Agrawal. She is of my CASTE. She is also in the design field. I can't believe that I decided to finally hook up. But it all happened so fast. She is a lovely girl, and I have been completely honest with her about everything. She has accepted me gracefully with

my past. Take care. Good Bye." Saanvi received a message on her mobile from Surya, abruptly one day.

Saanvi jumped with joy. There was a sign of relief she experienced. She was offloaded from her guilt of hurting Surya. She felt elated to know he would also have a partner in life who would do wonderful things for him just like she had in her life.

She called him on his mobile immediately with immense excitement in her voice, *"Hi. I am so so so so so so so so happy for you. I might be happier than you right now. You won't believe this, but I am jumping with joy, like literally. I wish you immense happiness with Pooja."*

"Thanks a lot, Saanvi. I am glad. You take care ok? Good Bye." He replied shortly and sweetly, as though he wasn't interested in extending the conversation.

'That was abrupt. He might be busy at work.' She thought to herself and didn't bother much.

Saanvi hadn't realized till then what the 'Goodbye' in his message had meant. It was a bye forever. It was a 'please don't keep in touch with me again, bye'. He didn't want to have any association with her anymore. He didn't want to complicate his new life with his old life. Henceforth, his friendship with Saanvi had to end.

She didn't realize this until a couple of months had passed. She kept messaging him, and he wouldn't reply. She kept thinking he must have been busy with wedding preparations, so she didn't bother much.

She lost patience and called him finally in October to wish him on his birthday. He didn't pick up her call. So, she left him a voice message.

"Hey, Surya. Happy birthday! Where have you been? Really busy, huh? Call back whenever you are free. By the way, I am planning to visit India in December so I thought of attending your wedding. Just let me know what the exact dates are. Cya."

Saanvi received a message back after a couple of hours. *"Hey. I have made a decision for myself. I can't keep in touch with you anymore. I am committed to Pooja and don't want my past to affect my future. I hope you will respect my decision."*

Saanvi didn't know how to react to this. She was happy for him, but losing him as a friend was not the price she had expected to pay. She had to accept his decision. After all, it was his turn to ditch her.

Saanvi gracefully carried on in her life with Ambar. She saw updates on Facebook of Surya's wedding and pictures of them as a couple. She congratulated him on Facebook but didn't receive any reply.

Saanvi's night awakenings gradually began again. She felt there was some void that could be filled in her life with a baby. Ambar agreed with her idea of trying to start a family.

LIFELESS JOURNEY

Dragging the burden of the unknown
lifelessly walking away
with no grief, no sigh
but neither a sign of happy ray.

It was obvious
it was fake
then why, may I ask,
and for whose sake?

Where is the spirit
and life of the charmer?
Or now is the journey lifeless
as I see, you chose to surrender?

That's not what is expected
'Be a fighter' is the answer
fight the destiny
test the tester.

'Coz from where I see
it is not the end
In fact, it's the beginning
'HOPE' is your new friend.

JUNE 2016

CHAPTER 6

SUPPRESSED EMOTIONS

A couple of years passed by trying for a baby, but there was no success. Not being able to start a family got her further depressed. Ambar and Saanvi visited a number of doctors and tried everything they possibly could. All tests, treatments, and medications failed. She had lost hope.

She resigned from her job as she was told that high stress levels sometimes become an obstacle. Her night awakenings increased further and further. She would wake up and look at Ambar and start crying. He would console her and cheer her up in every manner possible. The bubbly and cheerful Saanvi had been trapped away in the arms of sadness and depression.

"I think we need a holiday. Let's go to India. Aaaaa.....Kashmir. What say? I'll apply for leave. Then we'll visit your parents also on the way back. It'll be a

good break for us from all the stress." Ambar suggested it to Saanvi.

"That's a brilliant idea. I like it." She was thrilled.

A couple of months later, they flew down to Kashmir for a beautiful holiday. It was very romantic. Saanvi felt relaxed, and the gorgeous valleys and hills of Srinagar refreshed her with positivity. They met up with her parents back in her hometown.

Ambar left Saanvi and her mother to enjoy some quality time. He went out for a walk that evening.

"Ambar is a lovely boy. He just loves you so much and is always taking care of you. After so many years of marriage, he hasn't changed, which is so rare. Destiny brings us to the right person always." Sarita Ji expressed it with joy.

"Yes, Ma. You are right. He is really great. Perfect. Everything is fabulous. He treats me like a princess. Yet, I am not fully happy. I don't know why. I just want to cry most of the time. I know I shouldn't be telling you this. But I have to get it out of my system. Otherwise, it'll turn me mad. I still dream about Surya."

Saanvi's reply shocked Sarita Ji. *"What?"*

"I wake up from my sleep and recall my dream. Sometimes, I hang out in the garden with him.

Sometimes, I bring him tea. I know it's wrong. He has moved on and gotten married. I have such an amazing husband. Yet, this is happening to me for real. No matter how much I try, there is a small part of my brain that just doesn't want him to get released from my memories. It troubles me. But how can I control my dreams? They are not in my hands. Yes, I try never to think about him in my consciousness, but what do I do about my subconscious mind?" She opened-up wholeheartedly.

"Saanvi, Surya wasn't the guy for you. Haven't you realized it yet? How can you think such things?" Sarita Ji tried to make her realize.

"He could have been the guy for me if you hadn't refused. You didn't even give him a chance. He, too, would have loved me like this."

"Do you still regret this? If you do, you will be the only person in the whole world who is refusing happiness. You know Saanvi. You should value what you get. You are being served food on a silver plate, and yet you want to go beg on the streets for food."

"No, Ma. I do not regret anything. But I have a problem and I need your help to solve it. Else, these dreams will drive me crazy."

"Dreams are only dreams, dear. They never become real. Once your mind starts thinking about other

things, your dreams about Surya will disappear. You mentioned about starting a family. Focus on that now. It is genuinely the best solution. Once you have a baby all ridiculous thoughts of other boys will vanish into thin air."

Sarita Ji was oblivious to the mental state of Saanvi's subconscious mind. She was blinded by the societal norms and traditional value systems. No words of Saanvi made any sense to her.

THE UNHEARD VOICE

The voice – for a change
was loud and clear
but unheard and unknown
I guess, was the fear.

I knew it was familiar
but that wasn't satisfying
to make my anxiety
and my nervousness disappear.

Curiosity erupted
and pushed me to enquire,
is this some unique sense of feeling,
or an outcome of a mere desire?

The confusion blocked my progress
left me suppressed.
Soon, I realized I had missed my chance
and it was too late.

The time, the moment had passed.
Left were ashes of my own
the voice, now, slowly blurs away
and, I know one day it shall be gone.

But, deep down, I shall regret
for not being firm
to reassure my expression
and admit my true emotion.

Ambar got back. The conversation ended, leaving Saanvi thinking about how embarrassed she was to feel the way she had been feeling. She knew her mother was right. But hearing herself say it loud, the first time sharing it with somebody, she realized what an idiot she was. People would think she was crazy and disgusting if they ever knew how unfaithful she was being to Mr. Perfect, Ambar, although at a sub-conscious level.

A few days passed by with a lot of sight-seeing and socializing. A couple of days were left to head back to Paris when Saanvi requested Ambar, "*Can we please visit my College once before we head back? It'll just take a day trip. We'll fly to Ajmer in the morning and be back by evening. Is it ok?*"

"*Of course. We'll try to meet your college friends too,*" Ambar replied without any hesitation.

The intention of this trip to India was to cheer Saanvi up. He was ready to do whatever it took to do that. Sarita Ji hadn't liked this idea of revisiting Ajmer, especially after the conversation she had with Saanvi. She feared Saanvi would try to meet Surya. But she couldn't refuse them. She didn't have any valid reason to present her case to Ambar. Unwillingly, she had to approve them.

Saanvi, too, had no intention to reunite with Surya, especially after Surya had made it crystal clear to part ways.

Her only reason for proposing this was to go back to where her wonderful memories with Surya were connected. She had the idea to stroll onto her campus and meet her College professors after years. She also thought of catching up with other friends like Ananya and Karan.

12 AUGUST 2016

CHAPTER 7

BIG BANG

Ambar and Saanvi caught a flight to Ajmer in the morning the next day. The weather wasn't in favor of their trip. Even God has his own signs to tell us their wishes. Heavy rainfall was accompanied by thunder and lightning. They caught a cab directly to her campus. But it was so hazy and foggy that the driver could barely see beyond a few meters. The driver turned around to ask if he should head back to the airport as he thought it was too risky to drive further. Before Ambar could reply, they hit into a truck. All three of them jerked up and were severely injured.

The rear of the car was crushed. Broken glass pieces entered Ambar's body. Saanvi had lost consciousness due to a sudden, jerky hit to the roof of the car. A guy from the street called the ambulance. All three of them were admitted into the operation theatre. Fortunately, the driver survived with a minor fracture in his arm. But

Ambar and Saanvi were critical. Both of them had sunk into coma.

Saanvi's mobile flashed with a ring written 'Mom', and the nurse picked up the call. The nurse informed Sarita Ji about the accident. Both Sarita Ji and Saanv's Dad were in a state of shock.

"Both of them are in coma. Oh no!" she exclaimed.

Her hands were shaking as she packed a bag. *"I had a bad feeling about this. Saanvi shouldn't have decided to go there. That place is only cursed for us."* She, along with Saanvi's Dad rushed to the airport to catch a flight for Ajmer immediately.

On reaching the hospital, they went on to check on Ambar and Saanvi in the ICU. The Doctor guided them to their rooms.

"Mrs. Saanvi has had a deep head injury. She doesn't have any external injuries. In the past 12 hours of observation, her condition has improved. We are expecting her to regain consciousness in the next 24 hours. But I am a little concerned about her head injury. She may have some temporary memory loss due to shock. This is only an assumption. Just pray. Actually, we are a bit more concerned about Mr. Ambar. Glass pieces have entered his body and may have entered his arteries. His brain isn't responding. We need to operate on him again in a couple of days. But we can't say how

long it will take for him to recover from coma." the head neurosurgeon explained to both of them.

Sarita Ji stood lifeless. She was in so much shock that her tears had dried. She didn't know how to react. Her kids had come down for a holiday, and now they were fighting for their lives.

Waiting in the corridor of the hospital for the next 12 hours, Sarita Ji and Saanvi's father trembled with fear of losing their loved ones. Every minute was like an hour, and every hour was like a long day.

Saanvi's nurse ran to her parents: *"Patient is gaining consciousness. You can come in."*

Saanvi's eyes were opening slowly. The sudden brightness made her shut her eyes again. She saw the nurse first, and then she saw her mother. She opened her lips and struggled to say a few words, *"Ma….You here….. Surya?"*

She started breathing heavily and shut her eyes again.

Sarita Ji was shocked to hear the name Surya come from Saanvi's mouth. She didn't comprehend what had just happened. She asked the doctor.

"As I said earlier, she may have lost some time from her memory. I am not sure. We will have to wait." He replied. But her questions couldn't be answered

yet. She had to wait for Saanvi to wake up again to solve this mystery. A couple of hours later, Saanvi woke up properly with complete consciousness.

Her first question was, *"Where is Surya, Ma? I am having a headache."*

The Doctor asked her, *"Ok, dear. What is the last thing that you remember?"*

She replied with a question, *"Why am I in the hospital? What happened?"*

"You met with an accident. Do you recall?"

"Oh yes, right. I was on our project site with Surya, and something fell on me. It hit my head hard. It must have been a ceiling light. Is Surya ok?"

"Who is Surya?"

"My husband. Isn't he here?"

"Since when are you married?"

"12 years. Why? Where is he? Why are you asking me all this?"

"It's just some routine tests to check if all is ok. Do you know Ambar?"

"Not really. Why?"

"How old are you?"

"Thirty-two."

"Where do you stay?"

"Here, in Ajmer."

"With who?"

"I live here with Surya, my husband and my two-year-old daughter, Aashna. She is at home right now with our maid. We stay on Qualis street. My friends Ananya and Karan would be able to help you out. You can call them if something is wrong. Aahhhh… I have a headache, Doctor."

"Ok. Please take rest."

She shut her eyes. The doctor and Saanvi's parents proceeded outside the ICU towards his cabin. He showed them her brain scan reports and pointed at a particular part on the scan.

"Well, can you see this? This is the prefrontal lobe. The prefrontal cortex (PFC) is the cerebral cortex that covers the front part of the frontal lobe. This brain region has been implicated in planning complex cognitive behavior, personality expression, decision making, and moderating social behavior. Saanvi's prefrontal cortex is showing decreased activity. Usually, during most dreams, the person dreaming is not aware that they are dreaming, no matter how absurd or eccentric the dream is. The reason for this may be that the prefrontal cortex, the region of the brain responsible for logic and planning, exhibits decreased activity during dreams. This allows the dreamer to more actively interact with the dream without thinking

about what might happen, since things that would normally stand out in reality blend in with the dream scenery."

"What are you trying to say, doctor? Please explain in layman's terms. This is all too much science for us."

"Well, basically, sometimes the dreams we have seem so real. Most of the emotions, sensations, and images we feel and visualize are those that we can say we have seen or experienced in real life. This is because the same parts of the brain that are active when we are awake are also active when we are in certain stages of our sleep. Exactly the opposite of that, in Saanvi's case, all parts of the brain that are inactive during sleep and dreams are also inactive after she has woken up. All I am saying is that Saanvi has woken up in a dream. She must have had imaginative characters in her dream, and she has woken up to believe that her dream is her reality. All these names she took - Surya, Ananya, Pooja, her daughter Ashna are an outcome of her imagination."

"Well, her daughter is an imagination, but the other names are not. Surya, Ananya, and Pooja are her college friends."

"Oh, I see."

"Has she desired a child?"

"Yes. Ambar and Saanvi have been trying to have a baby for a couple of years now. And she remains depressed about not being able to conceive."

"And this Surya. Was she close to him in her past?"

"Aaaaa...yes. She thought she was in love with him back in college days. You know how young kids are! But it was over. Although a few days ago she mentioned to me that she, at times, has dreams about Surya."

"Yes. Exactly. I have understood the whole case now, at least, so I think. Basically, Saanvi, when in coma, must have had a long dream. Due to the continuously decreased activity of her prefrontal cortex, her dream lasted longer than a normal dream, about 15 to 20 minutes at most. She must have probably dreamt of all the things that she has desired for: her unfulfilled desires, like being married to Surya and having a child, working on some project and having a career, being closely in touch with college friends, etc. After waking up, her prefrontal cortex is still in the same condition as it was while dreaming. This is an unusual case and may have been a result of the damage caused to the brain during the accident. I haven't come across such a case in my career. But I had come across a case study a few years ago. I will refer to it to get a clearer picture. Meanwhile, we will keep her under observation."

"When will she recover, Doctor? What will we tell Ambar when he gains consciousness?"

"Well, honestly, such cases are very unpredictable. Any kind of surgery is not helpful. We can only try medication. We have to see how her body and mind react

to medication. Regarding Ambar, I am not sure when he will gain consciousness. But we will discuss that when that situation arises. As of now, let us focus on getting them back to normal health."

Saanvi woke up again after a few hours. In the hope of her being normal, Sarita Ji started telling her about Ambar, which might trigger her mind back to her normal real life: *"Ambar is still in coma. We have informed his parents."*

Saanvi replied, *"That's good. I think you should tell Surya also to talk to them. Is Surya ok? I haven't seen him since I got here. Give me my phone. I want to call him."*

Sarita Ji was in shock and desperate. *"Surya is not your husband. You are married to Ambar. Wake up, Saanvi. Wake up. Remember you live in Paris. You came here for a holiday."*

She thought that by telling her the reality, she might remember everything and get normal. But she was mistaken. Instead, Saanvi's pulse started dropping, and she became unconscious. The nurse went running to the doctor to call for help.

As soon as the doctor came in, Sarita Ji briefed him about what had happened. She explained that she was trying to help her get out of her dream. Little did she know that she had worsened Saanvi's case?

"Oh no, Madam. What did you do? I was just talking to our Head of Psychiatry department and briefing about Saanvi's condition. The first instruction that he gave me was not to reveal or let the patient realize that there is something wrong with them. Let them continue to believe what they believe. As stressing their nervous system now could be dangerous and risk their lives. The decreased activity could suddenly stop if we don't let her believe what she believes. This may lead to the patient shifting into a coma condition or even death. We need to be very careful, Ma'am. Please don't repeat this ever again. In fact, I would suggest that we call Surya and her friends here and explain to them the case and if they could help out, nothing like it."

"No way. We don't have any way to contact Surya. Moreover, I would not like to drag him into this. I have heard he is married and settled. This would affect his life. There has to be another way out, Doctor."

"Ok, then we try to stall Saanvi's questions about Surya and her dream life. But do not deny any of her beliefs. Let's see how it works."

A couple of days passed by. The doctors and Sarita Ji kept stalling Saanvi's questions about Surya and her daughter, Ashna.

18 AUGUST 2016

CHAPTER 8

BEGINNING OF THE END

Saanvi woke up past 10:30 pm on her hospital bed. She saw her mother sleeping on the couch next to her bed. She saw her mobile phone on the side table. She raised slightly in slow motion, taking care of the heaviness from her head, and picked up the phone. She dialed Surya's college time mobile number several times. But it kept saying, 'This number doesn't exist.' She got worried. She thought to herself, '*I think something has happened to Surya. No one is telling me about him. That's why he isn't coming here and now his number is not reachable. I need to look for him. I need to go home to check if he is okay. I have to see him and our daughter, Ashna.*'

Saanvi removed the drip tube from the needle hand, something she had picked up from watching a lot of Bollywood movies. She picked up her fresh clothes from the duffle bag that her Mom had brought. She changed into them, pulled out a few hundred rupees from her mother's purse and took her mobile phone, slowly walked out of the room inaudibly. She sneakily walked towards the main entrance, covering her face with a hospital mask. She smartly hid from the hospital staff and exited the hospital. It wasn't too difficult as the staff on night duty didn't recognize her much. She caught a cab to Surya's home address that she remembered from college time. She paid the cab guy his fare and hastily walked towards the door that was the entrance to Surya's home, located on the ground floor.

It was half past midnight and pouring heavily. Saanvi rang the doorbell. Surya, dressed in a baggy pair of shorts and a loose T-shirt opened the door. His hair was messy, and his eyes were half open, just woken up from a half-hearted sleep.

Saanvi looked at him, and tears rolled down her cheeks. She just bombarded him with agitation as she let herself in uninvited, *"Oh my God, you are fine! Thank God! Why is your phone switched off then? Where have you been? Why are you ignoring me? Why weren't you there at the hospital with me? Have we had a fight? Where is Ashna? I have such a bad headache. I don't remember much."*

Surya, taken aback by this bizarre and extremely awkward situation that had arisen, took a few steps backwards to comprehend what had just happened. He stared at her with curiosity and seemed completely nervous.

"Why are you staring at me as though I am a stranger? Is there something on my face? Were you busy, or are you angry with me? I know something is wrong; otherwise you would never do this. I was in the hospital for seven days and you didn't come to see me. Please tell me. You have never done anything like this ever since we got married."

Surya didn't have words to describe how amazed and startled he was. Yet, spontaneously he reacted with wisdom more than aggression or shock. *"You are shivering – here, take a towel. Wipe yourself. Relax, and please explain what's going on. I am super confused."*

A middle-aged, tall, pretty lady, Pooja, dressed in a long skirt and cute, short t-shirt with a 2-year-old kid in her arms came from the bedroom and called out, *"Who is it, honey?"*

"Aaaaaaaaaa...........It's.....Saanvi." He replied hesitatingly with a shiver in his trembling voice.

Saanvi pointed at Pooja and asked Surya who she was.

Pooja dived in and replied to Saanvi directly, *"I am his wife. Hi. We haven't met in all these years. But I have heard a lot about you. Glad to meet you finally."*

Saanvi froze. She bumped into a new character which did not fit into her imaginative world. She didn't understand what she had heard. Her head started wobbling on her neck, and her eyes began shutting. *"Surya, Surya,"* she called out and banged her head against the wall and fell down and became unconscious. The breakdown situation from the hospital had repeated.

Surya and Pooja stood still.

Pooja looked at Surya with inquisitiveness and immense confusion.

Surya looked equally baffled and explained to Pooja, *" Saanvi just walked in and behaved as if she was my wife. I didn't get anything. I think she is playing some prank on me. Perhaps Ananya and Karan know about something or it's probably their evil plan to break the ice between Saanvi and me. I am as shocked as you. Trust me!"*

He called them up and looped both of them on a conference call while Saanvi was still unconscious and asked them to stop playing this stupid prank. Both of them replied, stating that they didn't have any idea about what he was talking about. Infact, they didn't even know that Saanvi was back in town. He requested that they come over.

Meanwhile, the cell phone in Saanvi's hand rang. Surya picked up the phone. "*Hello.*"

"*Who is this?*" An aged lady's voice was on the other line.

"*Aunty? Are you Saanvi's mother? This is Surya.*"

"*Surya? Oh, is Saanvi with you?*"

"*Yes, aunty. What's happening? She just came in at my house a few minutes ago, and now she has fainted here.*"

"*Oh my God. Surya, please give me your address. We will be right there to get her.*"

"*It's house no. 22A, Qualis street, Arthur Road, Near M M A crossroads.*"

"*Ok, thank you. And don't wake her up. She may behave abnormally, and you may not be able to handle it. Apologies for any trouble.* "

"*No problem, aunty.*"

He told Pooja to help him carry Saanvi and keep her on the couch next to where she had fainted in the living room. "*Aunty has advised me not to wake her up. She said something about Saanvi behaving abnormally. I think something's wrong. Looks like it's not a prank after all.* "

Karan and Ananya also reached Surya's house and enquired, *"What happened, buddy? We swear we don't know anything. And after all that's happened in the past, do you think we'd play such a ridiculous prank?"*

Surya replied, *"Ya. Sorry guys. I just found out from Saanvi's mother. She is coming to pick up Saanvi. I think we'll learn further details once she gets here."*

An ambulance siren was heard gradually increasing in volume, and then it stopped at Surya's doorstep. Sarita Ji walked out along with a few hospital staff. A few neighbors peeped out of their balconies too, woken up by the siren.

"Hello, Surya. Oh, hello, Ananya and Karan. How are you all? I am sorry you had to go through all this trouble. Saanvi is not well. Need to take her back to the hospital."

Surya and Pooja looked at each other. Surya hinted to Pooja to go ahead and ask Aunty for the details.

"Aunty, let us know if we could be of any help. You look very worried. Saanvi is a friend, and we all would like to know what has happened to her. Clearly, she isn't ok." Pooja politely expressed her concern and query.

"Well, to cut a long story short, Saanvi and her husband met with a car accident. Ambar is in coma and Saanvi has had some neuro damage," Sarita Ji replied in haste and rushed out.

Surya couldn't resist himself and stopped Sarita Ji at the door. *"Aunty, I know I have no right to intrude, and you did make things very clear in the past. I haven't interfered in her life since then. But today, she has come to my doorstep after so many years and has called me her husband. Please share with me what has happened to her exactly and why is she behaving so oddly. She has involved me, and now I would appreciate if you would let me know more details."*

As much as his brain resisted, his heart couldn't hold himself from enquiring further details. Clueless about the future, he innocently swept himself into a mess he couldn't have imagined at all.

With a lot of stress and awkwardness, Sarita Ji replied hesitatingly, *"To be honest, there is nothing like that. I just didn't share more as I didn't want to disturb you and your family. However, since you ask, it is hard to say much, but the doctors are also trying to figure out what exactly has gone wrong. I am also not very sure about the details, but from her behavior ever since she woke up, we assume she has had a memory loss of reality and is stuck in some fictitious world where she feels she is married to you and has a kid with you. It is like she is literally* ***living in her dream.****"*

Pooja and Surya were zapped with this statement. Ananya and Karan also couldn't believe what they had heard. Ananya asked Sarita Ji when this happened and offered to join her to the hospital.

Karan, Pooja and Surya stayed back. They kept silent for a couple of minutes, wondering how they should address this issue. Little did they know that the decision they were about to take was going to change Surya and Pooja's lives forever.

"This is such a weird situation. What do you plan to do now, Surya?" Karan asked.

"What do you mean? What should I plan? What can I do in this situation? Doctors have to take care of this. Not me," Surya responded spontaneously.

"I think you should visit the hospital and check on Saanvi. Ask Aunty about the exact situation. Maybe you can be of some help to them in reminding Saanvi of the reality," Pooja suggested.

Surya was annoyed but at the same time amazed with Pooja's maturity. His wife was asking him to help out his ex-girlfriend. *"Are you crazy? You want me to help Saanvi. You know how complicated all this is, right?"*

"Of course, I know. I am not playing dumb here. But this is not an obsessed freak who has come back into our lives. This is a medical condition. Talking to you may trigger her to get better sooner than how the doctors may handle her case. I have faith in you, and helping her out doesn't make you less loyal," She urged.

"I think Pooja is right. It is a great gesture by you. Surya, come on, at least let's go to the hospital and figure out what is going on." Karan added.

"If they need my help, they will tell me. Plus, it is not a question of my loyalty towards my marriage. You know that I have ended all connections with Saanvi for a reason, and now going down that road again just is very awkward and feels wrong." Surya expressed his reluctance clearly.

"If you were in Saanvi's place and Saanvi was in yours, wouldn't she reach to you to help you out?" Karan insisted. Pooja supported him as well and pushed Surya to say what he was about to say.

"Pooja, baby, make sure you stand by me in every situation, and always remember you are pushing me to take this step into this complicated scenario. Once I enter, there will be no looking back. No matter how weird and awkward it gets, we will face it together." Surya confirmed.

Pooja nodded and hugged Surya with a big smile to comfort him. She wants to do the right thing and help Saanvi in the situation.

Karan and Surya rode down to the hospital in Karan's car. Karan sensed the discomfort and anxiety in Surya's eyes. He himself wasn't sure how all this was going to pan out. But he knew that at this point, this was the human thing to do for an old friend's sake.

Surya shared his reluctance once again with Karan, *"I know this is the right thing to do, but I am very scared. Saanvi was a closed chapter in my life. And this whole situation is just so bizarre, so crazy. What am I supposed to do when I see her now?"*

Karan handled him maturely. *"Well, for starters, let us first meet Saanvi's doctor. Find out the actual medical condition. And if at all your presence in front of her is going to be of any help or not. For all we know, the doctor may say you are not needed. Or he might say that you need to remind her that both of you aren't married. Let's see."*

They reached the hospital and called Ananya to locate the room Saanvi was in. Surya opened the door of the room and looked at Saanvi lying unconscious. His past memories rushed into him, and he had a brain freeze. He didn't want to go down that road again, he thought to himself. It was a dangerous lane filled with mixed emotions. His heart and brain weren't supporting each other, and this troubled him immensely. He put himself together and called Saanvi's mother out to discuss the next steps.

He requested Sarita Ji to step out for a bit to have a word. *"Aunty, what do the doctors say? Is there anything that I am required to do? Please don't hesitate if you need my help."*

Saanvi's mother couldn't believe her ears. The boy whom she had rejected years ago was present there to help them out of this situation in spite of their past negative encounter. Her eyes were filled with tears of guilt and gratitude.

She joined her hands toward Surya and apologized, *"I am so sorry. I misread your character years ago. You are a gentleman to have come here to help us out. It is very kind of you. I was wrong about you. Please forgive me for misjudging you at that point. If I had not refused your alliance with Saanvi at that point, she wouldn't have suffered all these years. She wouldn't be in this state today, neither here nor there, away from reality; her mind trying to live her desired life, which is unreal. I regret my decision so much. I regret killing her and your emotions thinking about other aspects of society. The heart wants what it wants, and I was no one to ruin that for both of you. Both of you had to go separate ways because of me. Ambar is a gem but he is not you."* She burst out crying and sat down on the chair.

Surya was numb. He couldn't respond to this for a few seconds. His life had flipped because of this woman standing in front of her. He had wished for this day to come for years. Finally, it happened. Sarita Ji's apology and realization relieved him of his anger. He felt liberated in that very instant. He had watery eyes, but he controlled himself.

Surya forgivingly held her by the shoulder and consoled her, *"Aunty, bygones are bygones. Everything is destined. We weren't meant to live together in spite of the strong feelings we had for each other. Don't hold yourself responsible. My life was supposed to be spent with Pooja and Saanvi's with Ambar. What Saanvi is facing now is just a medical condition. When she is out of it, everything will be fine. We will do whatever it takes to get her back to normal and get her back to reality. She has to get back to normal for Ambar."*

Sarita Ji wept rigorously after witnessing Surya's unimaginable kindness. Her guilt encompassed her lifelong judgment. She had been so wrong to reject Surya. Her preconceived ideology about intercultural marriage was questionable. Her daughter's choice wasn't wrong after all. She finally got a chance to learn what Saanvi had seen in Surya. Why couldn't she just trust Saanvi's gut feeling? She stared at Surya with apology in her eyes. She wished she could have turned back time. She thought to herself, *'This boy is so sorted; he has shown so much maturity, not only now but back then as well. He could have easily convinced Saanvi to take drastic measures like eloping with him, but he didn't. He respected us and our decision in spite of it not being in his favor. He backed off then, and he is handling today's scenario also so well. Sometimes, as parents, we are so clouded by our ridiculous societal pressures that we don't let our children take certain correct decisions.'*

Anyway, her realizations were too late. Things were different now, and turning back time was an impossible technology in the current scenario.

Ananya rushed out and informed, *"Saanvi has regained consciousness."*

Surya and Sarita Ji sprinted in. Saanvi looked at Surya and asked him to come closer. *"Don't play pranks with me ever again. You know I can't accept even if someone jokes about being your wife. By the way, who was that lady with our kid? I can't recall her. Is she a new friend?"*

Surya calmly tried to remind her about reality versus her fantasy. "*Saanvi, you and I have never gotten married. That lady is my wife, Pooja, and you are married to Ambar. You live in Paris with him. Both of us haven't seen each other in years. You are hallucinating, my dear.*"

Saanvi began breathing heavily, listening to these facts. Her brain was rejecting them. She started shaking fiercely, and her body was getting cold. Her eyes started shutting slowly, and her pulse fell to dangerously low levels. The doctors rushed in and began working on her.

Surya was zapped with her reaction. His attempt to remind her of facts was not only futile but was life-threatening for Saanvi. He had tears in his eyes. He couldn't believe what had happened. He left the ward and cried tremendously outside in the hall. Karan hugged Surya for a long time until he finally calmed down.

Surya shared his feelings with Karan, "*Saanvi is still in love with me, Karan. After so many years, her mind doesn't want to accept that I am not with her. Although a result of a medical condition, these are all unresolved feelings surfacing. She is like a pressure cooker now. Refusing to undo what she believes is true. What do I do? How do I solve this issue? Where has destiny brought us all? Can't believe this situation; I……I……I….." and he starts crying again."*

Karan didn't have words of consolation this time. This was such an odd and never-heard-of situation. The usual problem solver, Karan, was also in a complete state of shock and at a loss for words and ideas this time. He continued to hug Surya. This was the only remedy he could bring to the table for now.

Ananya joined both of them for a group hug. Her mind was the sanest of the rest of them. *"I think let's discuss with the doctor how this whole situation needs to be handled. Let's not get dejected. When there is a problem, it has a solution. We just need to find it. Surya, please calm down. I know it is too much to ask right now. But you are the key to this entire lock fixed on Saanvi's mind. And you will have to act exactly according to the doctor's advice to unlock this. I know it will be hard, very hard. But it is for Saanvi. And clearly, she has not stopped loving you to date. So, let's all stay calm and handle it with sanity."*

The doctor came out. *"Patient is stable for now but is unconscious. I would like to speak to the family and Mr. Surya. Could you follow me, please?"*

They all went to the doctor's cabin as he started explaining, *"So it's good you tried to remind her of the facts, but it didn't work; rather, it has put her brain in further shock. This could probably be due to the fact that her dream is now her reality. I am still unsure of how we will bring her back to reality. But as of now, we have to let her believe what she thinks is true. You all will have to pretend the roles that she thinks are true. Let us all go with the flow. We need her brain to have some time to process reality. It may happen one day all of a sudden or gradually with time when her factual memory slowly starts coming back in. We all need to be patient. I know, Mr. Surya, this is too much to ask from you, but would it be possible for you to pretend to be her husband for a few days?"*

Sarita Ji looked with guilt in her eyes towards Surya, hoping he would say yes and simultaneously feeling so bad that he is going to be in this situation. She had to be selfish for her daughter.

Surya responded, *"Doctor, I would like to help out in any manner possible. But I am not just myself. I have a wife and a kid. And my wife's consent is more important than mine. Also, I find it very unethical to bring her into all of this. Why should she have to deal with any of this? Couldn't we find another solution?"*

The doctor replied with regret, *"Well, I understand your situation. And it is completely justified. You already gave the other solution a shot, and clearly, it only worsened the scenario. Just see if it is possible. I don't see another option as of now. Let's wait for Saanvi to gain consciousness and see her reaction. You can decide after that."*

After three and a half hours, Saanvi woke up. Surya prayed for her to have gotten back to reality so that this roller coaster ride of emotions could end for him, but God had something else written for them.

Saanvi asked Sarita Ji for Surya. He came in. She looked at him with a smile on her face. Her smile had a satisfaction and her eyes were glowing with a tear in the corner. *"Sit next to me please. You know, I feel like I haven't seen you for so long. Your face, your eyes, your smile; I just want to keep looking at you for as long as possible. Please don't go away."*

Surya asked her, *"How are you feeling?"*

She replied, *"I have a headache and feel a little disoriented. Also, my back hurts just from lying in the bed for so long. Rest all ok. Ask the doctor, till when do I have to be here. I am tired of the hospital food. I want to go back home. "*

Surya kept his hand on her head and said," *You had a major accident, Saanvi. The doctor said it would take a few days to get better. We have to listen to the doctor, ok? You want to get completely okay, right?"*

Although pretending, his care for Saanvi was just like in the past. His warmth was what Saanvi was looking for. She had missed this for so many years. Although her brain didn't remember, she somewhere deep down did feel alive with his presence.

She expressed to him, *"You know, I don't know why but I am feeling very happy right now. I feel like I haven't been so happy and relieved in a very long time. Maybe, I am seeing you after 7 days that's why. Please stay next to me always ok. I will get better with your hand in my hand automatically. I love you so much."*

Surya held Saanvi's hand and smiled at her. He had tears rolling down his cheeks uncontrollably. He didn't have words. How could he tell her that it hadn't been 7 days but nearly 7 years?

She asked him, *"Hey…What happened? Why are you crying so much?"*

He said, *"Nothing. I just pray you get better soon. I will just go ask the doctor about your further treatment and get back soon."*

Saanvi's undying love for Surya was evident to him now. He thought to himself that he had been wrong about Saanvi all these years. He had always kept a grudge within himself. He had thought Saanvi was never serious enough in their relationship. That is why she never put up a fight with her parents for their love to last longer. He finally forgave her. He got closure.

What next? Surya was in the largest dilemma. His heart was torn in two. Should he stay back and continue this pretend play until the doctor tells him to? Or forget about all this and get to his wife and kid and live his own life?

Sarita Ji had also heard Saanvi's words.

The irony of the situation was that the life of her daughter was now in the hands of the boy she had rejected for her with complete insensitivity.

She joined her hands to Surya with pleading eyes and then walked away.

Pooja walked in towards Surya. She gave her kid to Ananya and hugged Surya tight. The understanding she was showing in this entire incident was remarkable. Surya was about to share with her the entire situation. But she interrupted him and told him that Ananya had already briefed her.

"What do you want to do? You know I will stand by your side and hold your hand in whatever decisions you take," she assured him.

He was taken aback by her kindness and generosity.

"You are the best wife and an excellent human being. Honestly, I don't know what I should do next. It would be so unfair to you if I helped Saanvi and pretended to be her husband. But it would damage her further if I didn't help her. She is nobody to me. But out of humanity, I feel I should help her. The doctors say this is the only way currently. But what do you have to say about this?" He expressed his confused state of mind.

Pooja was very compassionate. She told Surya to go ahead with whatever it takes to get Saanvi back to normalcy. *"I trust you. I know you love me. And you will never do anything that will hurt me. What you are about to do is pure help to a patient. So please don't be in such a dilemma and go ahead and follow the doctor's instructions."*

Before Surya could make up his mind and take a stand, the doctor came to Surya and asked to talk to him privately. *"There are some new developments that I would like you to review before taking a decision, Mr. Surya. Saanvi's cerebral activity has shown some development in the last two hours, just after she met you. We feel her interaction with you has been a positive development in her condition. I urge you to continue communication with her."*

Surya was convinced. He was going to help Saanvi in this situation, purely out of humanity. But in this process, there was one major battle he would have to face. He would have to fight his natural instincts of falling in love with Saanvi again while he helped her out. Deep down, he knew this at a subconscious level but decided not to let this fear become an obstacle in this act of humanity. He had the complete support of Pooja too.

They waited it out for a couple of hours. Meanwhile, Pooja told Surya that I am going to head home to make room for Saanvi's stay in their house. She would have to remove all photo frames hanging on the walls of their family so that there would be no chance of Saanvi getting stressed again. Also, they discussed what role Pooja would play, in their house for Saanvi to believe why she stays with them. Surya suggested that she could pretend to be my cousin's wife, who has been staying with us since my cousin works out of the country. Also, Gudiya (their daughter) got attached to you because Saanvi has been hospitalized for so many days, and you took care of her.

"Yes, this makes perfect sense. It is believable. Wow. This was quick thinking," Pooja approved.

The nurse came out asking for Surya. *"Patient has gained consciousness and is calling Surya. Sir, please come with me."*

Surya followed the nurse with turmoil inside him and a pretend smile on his face. How would he go through with this without getting attached to Saanvi again? All his feelings for her - love or hate - had to be put aside like a robot and he had to behave like an actor in a movie who will be living a life of pretense for the next few days/ weeks just as an act of charity for his ex-girlfriend (but the love of his life).

He went towards Saanvi with anxiety and tried to be very calculative in his moves and gestures. Saanvi held his hand. *"Why am I feeling so tired even when I wake up from sleep every time? I am not hurt anywhere; still, I feel heavy and burdened. What did the doctor say? What is wrong? Am I okay? Why are they keeping me here? Please don't hide anything. Tell me honestly what is going on."*

Ironically, that was the one thing he couldn't do - tell her honestly what was going on.

He calmed her down by patting her forehead with warmth. *"Relax. You are perfectly fine. Just after your accident you were in coma for a few days. But now you are ok. The doctor has kept you here to perform some tests before discharging you. Once reports arrive, we are going home."*

"Got it. Please stay by my side. Don't leave me again. I just don't want to be without you ever anymore."

She was saying words that weren't possible in reality, and yet Surya had to agree to them for now.

Surya told her only one person is allowed in the hospital during nights, and he should go home to their daughter, so only her Mom would stay with her. She accepted that excuse. He told her he has to work and give time to their baby but reassured her that he will visit her everyday although not for too long. She wasn't too happy about it, but she was convinced. At least she was going to see Surya every day.

The next day, Surya came in with flowers for her. He sat on the chair near her. She held his hand and said, *"You know, the only thing I am looking forward to in this hospital is meeting you. It is like I am asleep, and I wake up with a fear that I won't be seeing you ever again. It is so funny. Why would that happen? But I am constantly scared. We must have been together for so many years, yet my love for you is just the same as what it was back in college days. I really love you so much.*

And I think this accident has made me realize this a lot more. I can't imagine a life without you."

She had lived so many years without him. She had spent no time with him in the real world. But in her world of dreams (which she was living in reality now), she must have lived a whole life with him.

She held his hand and began to excitedly recall some bizarre moments, *"Remember, when both of us were in Kashmir? You pulled me and we rolled down the snow hugging each other. When I am out of here, I want to relive that with you. I want to be in your arms in the chilled snow again."*

He was compelled to agree to her but was internally feeling very awkward. She gently pulled him closer to her and kissed him on his forehead. He pulled away slowly and said, *"You need rest. Don't think so much. Relax."*

She felt the discomfort Surya had expressed. She could see a lack of passion for her in his eyes. She knew deep down that she was forcing herself on him. He told her that he had to leave for work and would come to visit her in the evening. She thought to herself, 'probably he is agitated with me for something that I can't recall.' She decided she was going to confront him that evening.

Surya stepped out, feeling heavy. His heart had to fight all his natural instincts of intimacy with her. He wasn't an actor. How long was he going to be able to pretend? He went into the doctor's cabin and expressed his issue. *"I can't do this, Doctor. I can't. I can't. I can't. I can't. I can't. I can't. I feel like I am betraying her. I am next to her but can't be with her. She shows her love, and I can't reciprocate it. But I have to pretend to reciprocate partly. I am not a Tom Cruise here. This isn't my job. This isn't a movie. This is reality. There are feelings involved. And not only hers. Mine and my wife's, as well. Everything she says to me in her dreamy fantasy world affects me. Please figure out another medical solution for her. I want to help, but this way isn't possible. She kissed me. I felt like I had cheated on my wife. Please understand."*

Surya had said all this in a single breath with rushed emotions. He wanted to just scream, but he didn't. The doctor showed him the brain scan (MRI) of Saanvi. He explained, *"We have tried a lot with her before you came into the picture. But nothing was working out. Her brain has shown a huge development. Do you see this? They are cells in a shifted state now due to the accident. We observed a movement in them when she met you, and after that, we monitored her for a few days when she was in the hospital. Your presence is stimulating her brain cells. It is not just emotions behind my request to you to continue this act, it is Science. Frankly, you are the only person who can help her with this. No one else."*

Surya was helpless. Torn by morals and emotions. His eyes spoke a million words as he stared at the doctor. And then he shut them softly, took a deep breath and released his pressure.

This has to be done, and there isn't an option, and he took it up as a challenge. *"Ok, I am going to do everything in my power to be there for her. This may have been meant to happen. Everything happens for a reason. I can't see it now, but I shall focus on getting her back to herself. She has to stop living in her dream and get back to reality."*

He finally agrees to take Saanvi home. It was going to be a new chapter in the life of all three of them. And none of them knew how long this was going to last.

21 AUGUST 2016

CHAPTER 9

FAKE REALITY

Life is full of surprises and shocks. People live in and out of them easily. Their minds are trained to do so since childhood. But no one is trained to live in someone else's dream world. To pretend to live a virtual reality. And not in Science fiction but an emotional battle. Surya and Pooja had to welcome an unwanted guest into their lives. They were the only hope left for Saanvi to revive. But how? No one, including the doctor, knew what that one trigger would be that could help Saanvi snap out of her imaginative reality into the real world of her husband. It was all on a trial-and-error basis. However, in this process of reviving Saanvi, wouldn't Surya and Pooja's relationship and settled life get disrupted? What kind of test was this?

Saanvi entered Surya's home with her Mom. Sarita Ji was speechless by their gesture of kindness. It is rare to see such humanity exist. She expressed her gratitude with folded hands and tears in her eyes. Pooja welcomed them with water. *"Please have a seat, Aunty. Please come, Saanvi. I'll take you to your room. Get comfortable and take rest."*

Saanvi exclaimed with sarcasm, *"So sweet of you to take so much care, but I think you are forgetting this is my house, and you are the guest, dear. It is your kindness that you have taken care of Ashna and Surya for this period, but I think now that I am back, feel free to carry on with your routine life."*

This came as a complete shock to all of them. Saanvi's reaction was totally unreasonable. But in her dream, Pooja wasn't a part of her life, and she was just waiting to eliminate this character from her virtual reality.

Pooja felt hurt but handled it well. She reverted, *"Oh yes, I know my dear – this is your home. But the doctor has said that you should not take the stairs for a while, so we have moved your room from upstairs to downstairs. And also, I live here only with you. I think you forgot. Maybe because of the accident. I am working in the same city and have been living here with you guys for a few months. So, don't worry about my routine. It is handled. Also, my presence will be useful as doctor has advised that you should not get too stressed physically."*

Sarita Ji took Saanvi to her room. She patted her cheek. *"Listen, dear. Behave well. Be kind to all. Especially Pooja. She is really a wonderful girl. She has done a lot for you ok? You may have forgotten. It is your duty to reciprocate her kindness and help with gratitude instead of being so rude."*

"Mom, I don't understand what she has done for me. In fact, I don't like her over niceness and sweetness. Feels fake. Who is she? Trying to take my place in the lives of Surya and Ashna. She took care of them for a couple of weeks and is behaving like she is the boss of the house. I am wondering how this is acceptable. Anyway, if you insist, I guess I can tolerate her for a couple of weeks till I get better," Saanvi expressed her strong disdain.

Saanvi was coming out to be the villain in the current scenario. Instead of expressing gratitude, she had shown clear signs of jealousy itself. This was a huge let down in the eyes of Surya. He looked at Pooja apologetically. He knew this was going to happen but didn't expect it to happen so soon. Saanvi was extremely insensitive. Since when did she become so heartless? She was so kind, always. Always polite and humble. Well, he hadn't seen her for years, and time changes people. Was it time or was it her unfulfilled desire to be with him which had turned her into this nasty, bitchy, jealous psycho? He kept having innumerable to and fro moments. Should he continue with this humanity exercise now or not?

Whilst he struggled with these apprehensions, to his surprise, Saanvi came up to Pooja and apologized. *"I am really sorry, Pooja. I was very insensitive. It is just that I am feeling like an outsider, you know. I was rude to you, probably because I was being jealous. So stupid of me to feel this way. You are such a sweetheart. I will cherish your kindness. We would love to have you here all the time. Please don't take what I said earlier to heart."*

Game changer.

Surya and Pooja were surprised as well as shocked at the same time by the sudden new avatar of Saanvi. Was this a game plan of Saanvi? Or was she truly into self-analysis? Surya knew Saanvi's core nature. He felt her apology was genuine and decided to forgive her.

Sarita Ji asked Surya if she should stay. Surya politely said, *"Aunty, however you are comfortable. You are most welcome to stay. But don't worry if you want to leave too. We are there for her. We can call you if we need anything too. Uncle may need you."*

Before Sarita Ji could react, Saanvi reached out, *"Mom. I am fine now. Don't worry about me. I am in my home. Surya loves me too much and will take care of me. Don't worry at all. You go with Dad. I will call you if I need anything."* Saanvi did not want her mother's interference anymore.

Sarita Ji felt it was appropriate to leave. The situation was awkward enough for Surya. She didn't want to complicate it further. She joined hands and left with gratitude and apology together in her eyes.

Surya went into Saanvi's room to see if she needed anything. Saanvi was sitting down and had frozen for a few seconds. She kept staring at the floor, and her smile had vanished. It was like her mind was blocked. Surya called out, *"Saanvi, are you okay?"* He shook her.

She startled and looked at him. As though she had just woken up. He repeated if she was ok. She looked at him again. She blinked her eyes. Then gave a short smile. She took a deep breath and expressed her dilemma. *"You know, Surya. I love you so much. But I am feeling lost. This is my home. But I feel like I don't belong here. I should be happy to be back home. But I am not feeling like I have lived here. This is all mine, I know. But I feel like nothing is mine. You must feel I am going crazy. But I am feeling disoriented. I remember seeing myself sleep here on this bed, but I can't remember how it felt. I am not sure if what I am saying is making sense anymore."*

Surya saw this as an opportunity to jog her memory.

"Do you remember Paris?" He enquired.

"Why suddenly Paris? Did we go there for a holiday?"

"You have lived there. You know that?"

"When did we live there?"

"Not we. Just you."

"Just me. Before we got married?"

"Yes."

"No, I don't remember. I remember us getting married just when we were in College. So, when did I live there?"

"What do you remember about our wedding?"

Saanvi suddenly had a big smile as she started describing that day: *"I remember you coming in a royal chariot, and I was in a doli. My eyes met your eyes. I could see a smile in your eyes. You looked like the happiest man on earth. I could see myself in your eyes. I could see our future together in your eyes. I remember having moist eyes too. I had tears of joy, you know. I was going to be with you for the rest of my life. We exchanged garlands. Circled around the fire. Took our vows. It was beautiful and surreal. Feels unreal now."* Ironically it was all unreal only.

She hugged him, and he hugged her back. He had tears in his eyes. He couldn't stop himself. It was an outburst.

"Why are you crying, Surya? What happened? Did I hurt you in any way?"

"Nothing. It's just that you have such a beautiful memory of a very special day."

A day that never existed in their lives. But she had probably lived it in her dreams multiple times.

They kept hugging each other for a few minutes. Surya kept crying. Saanvi kissed his forehead and wiped his tears. Surya smiled. He excused himself and said that he'd just go check on their daughter Ashna.

He went upstairs and saw Pooja playing with Ashna. He went and hugged Pooja. He cried again and continued to cry. Words weren't needed for any explanation for his trauma. They both knew why Surya was crying. Pooja understood him.

She had known about his past. It had taken him years to get over Saanvi. And now, her getting back in his life like this was going to be a huge emotional challenge for him.

Pooja had known how important Saanvi was to Surya. So, she was not going to question Surya about his outburst. She just patted him, expressing her love and understanding.

A few moments later, she cried herself. She began foreseeing where this situation was leading. And it didn't seem pleasant for her. Pooja realized Surya was going to get into a trap of emotions and get torn down between both women in the house.

Her kindness was going to turn the tables against her. But her greatness was in letting destiny play its role. *'Everything that happens, happens for a reason. We don't see it now, but the bigger picture will uncover itself when its time. Until then, we stay patient.'*

28 AUGUST 2016

CHAPTER 10

IT'S ALL AWKWARD

A week of Saanvi's dream life turning into reality had passed. Her presence and intrusion into every little thing in the house had started annoying Pooja. Pooja's patience was getting tested. Saanvi, too, wanted a lifetime of companionship with Surya. But Pooja was beginning to look like the thorn in her happy family picture with Surya and Ashna. To her, Pooja was nothing but an obstacle.

Surya had been sleeping in the guest room. He excused himself from sleeping with Saanvi, saying that he works up late in his study and the doctor hasn't permitted them to disturb Saanvi's sleep. And that is essential for her speedy recovery. To avoid any awkward encounters with the two women, Surya would rush to work as early in the morning as possible and return later in the night. He was restricting his conversations with everyone in the house to dinner table chats only.

Saanvi was tired of not getting time with Surya at all. She felt anxious as she began to have a void. She wondered if this was the life she had been living even prior to the accident. Her life felt hollow.

Pooja would keep to herself, her household work and her daughter. Saanvi would try to take control over household chores and take care of Ashna but she felt helpless every time she attempted to do something. She didn't remember what went where. She didn't seem to have any connection with the home. And she surely didn't have any bonding with Ashna.

Pooja would tell her not to worry. It is because of the accident that Saanvi is disoriented, and it would take time for her to get back her complete memory. Pooja would keep trying to make attempts to remind Saanvi of her past.

"Saanvi, do you have any memory or moment that you have with Ashna? Please share with me. I would love to hear. It may help you to trigger your memory." Pooja attempted to trigger Saanvi to realize that she didn't fit here.

Saanvi was about to revert instantly, feeling she obviously must have something, but she went blank. She tried hard to remember delivering her child or being pregnant with Ashna but failed to recollect a single moment. She couldn't even have a faint image of Ashna's birth or first steps or her first cry or first smile. She struggled to say something. But she was left with a lack of words. She couldn't even fake a memory at that moment as she was left in shock.

"Isn't it strange that you have memories with Surya but not with Ashna?" Pooja enquired.

Saanvi wasn't pleased with this inquiry by Pooja. She felt cornered. Her dislike towards Pooja grew stronger. Simultaneously, it struck her that she was completely disconnected from Ashna. She was compelled to ask herself if she truly was her mother. She had had an accident and some memory issues, but Ashna didn't. Why wasn't Ashna wanting to be with her mother? Also, Saanvi didn't feel obsessed about Ashna as a mother. Her heart would skip a beat only for Surya. Her anxiety was only for Surya. All these questions were raised in her mind with that one question from Pooja.

She called her friend Ananya and requested her to take her to the Doctor. *"I have to understand what is happening to me. I feel my life has become a joke. I feel so many things are hidden from me in this house. I am unaware of most things in my own house. My only daughter is completely disconnected from me. She actually plays with me like I am an Aunt, not her mother. I feel the doctor should have a few answers."*

The Doctor performed a few brain scans and checked if there was any change in her medical condition. He had hoped that in case there was any improvement, he would tell her the partial truth gradually. But it was not advisable in the current scenario. The best he could do is advise her to sleep well, take regular medication and not take any kind of stress. He explained the same to Ananya as well and told her to make sure that Saanvi isn't taking any stress.

Ananya, herself, was puzzled. It was obvious that if Saanvi's rational queries weren't answered, she was going to get stressed. Moreover, Surya, Pooja, and Ashna's family was going to continue to get disturbed. She felt like telling Saanvi everything but didn't want to be responsible for anything that went wrong as a result. She advised Saanvi to go live with her mother for a few days or just to take a break from all this and visit a tourist place for a holiday.

Ananya's advice actually backfired. Saanvi took her advice too seriously but in the wrong way. She went home and, during dinner, came up with the great proposal. *"I went to see the doctor. He advised me not to take any kind of stress so I could recover sooner. So Ananya came up with the idea that I need a holiday. I loved her idea. I really need to get away from all of this anxiety. Surya let us both, along with Ashna, go on a holiday to some mountains for a few days. The fresh air might help me heal."*

Pooja's first reaction was, *"Not Ashna! She can't."*

"Why not?"

Pooja had to formulate a believable lie for the sake of Ashna. She was so engaged in saving Ashna that she forgot that in that process, she was about to accept Saanvi's idea of a getaway alone with her husband, Surya. *"You had only told me Ashna has breathing trouble in the mountains and high-speed winds."*

Saanvi wasn't as disappointed as she should have been. She immediately switched by suggesting a holiday for just the two of them. *"I am sure Pooja will help out with Ashna for a few days as she always has been doing. At least let us both go, Surya. We really need this."*

Surya tried to dodge with multiple excuses of excessive work, doctor's approval for Saanvi's health, Ashna's care, Saanvi's mother's worry, etc."

But Saanvi was adamant. She made a puppy face and requested Surya once again, *"I know you are very worried with multiple things. But please trust me, this holiday will be very beneficial for my recovery. I have a strong gut feeling. I wouldn't insist so much otherwise. I know that is your top priority right now, my recovery. I feel helpless and lost here. Just for 3 to 4 days. Not much. Please. Pooja, please convince Surya. He listens to you a lot."*

Surya's heart started to race faster than ever. He started staring at Pooja. Nervousness was evidently trickling down his face in the form of perspiration.

"Look! Look how stressed you are. You need a break too. We both need some time together. It's final we are going. No discussion. Thanks so much, Pooja, for taking care of Ashna, as always. You are a sweetheart. Yaaay, I am so excited. I am going to call a travel agent to give options for holiday."

Surya and Pooja were stuck in an awkward silence. Surya, of course knew how inappropriate this was. But subconsciously felt happy for Saanvi's happiness. There was a time he could die for her smile. He could have easily stopped everything that was about to happen, but on some level, he probably didn't want to now. He looked at Pooja and raised his eyebrows. Pooja gasped. She knew she didn't have any escape from this. If Surya avoids this, it is correct. But if she said anything, it would make her feel guilty. She stood up and left without any words or expressions.

Surya's choice at this moment was going to alter his future forever. He had to choose Saanvi or Pooja. It was a straightforward choice to make. The room he would go to was the choice he was going to make. He closed his eyes and breathed deeply. His legs were shaking. He thought to himself, *"I should have just said a NO. Why didn't I? Pooja will understand. Of course, she won't. Does that mean I want to go with Saanvi? Would that be fair? But I want to be with her. It's wrong, but still, I want to. Oh no. Just what I had feared is happening."*

There are moments when 'the right' is superseded by 'unfulfilled desires and emotions'. Surya was tired of controlling his suppressed feelings. He walked upstairs to Pooja. *"I think it might be a good way to get rid of Saanvi if we go on this trip."*

"How so?"

"I will make sure she begins to dislike me and realizes that we are not together. We were never together."

"Why can't you do that here? Is a getaway mandatory?"

"She is uncomfortable here. She feels that is the reason it is not the same between us. I need her to know that it is all finished between us even if both of us are alone."

"I don't agree with you. But if you feel this is correct, I won't stop you. Do what you feel is best. I trust you. That is what matters to me."

"I know this sounds stupid. But I am proud of you for trusting me. And proud that we have built this relationship over these years. Thanks a lot."

Surya couldn't believe Pooja agreed so fast. *'How could she be so kindhearted and generous and trusting? She is such a gem. I will not break her faith in me. I have to make sure I do what I have told her. Oh God, give me the strength to fight my desires if I have any.'* Surya promised to himself.

1 SEPTEMBER 2016

CHAPTER 11

DREAMS FULFILL

THE UNSAID

Sunny sky, lit up farms,
cold winds, warm arms,
shut eyes, whispers in ears
why didn't we live this all these years?

Moments to make
which no one can break,
priceless and fearless
Could life be like this without stress?

Unfulfilled dreams and desires
buried under the fires
shall get a chance to ignite
when you and I will unite.

The unsaid shall be told
words in my heart that I hold
will flow out of me playing guitars
and sparkle your eyes like a million stars.

Saanvi and Surya were entering the car to head for their short getaway to Mt. Neshville, about 3 hours of drive from where they lived.

Surya's eyes couldn't move away from Pooja. They were simultaneously asking for forgiveness and requesting approval. It must take immense strength and confidence for Pooja to let Surya take this step. Somewhere, probably, deep down, Pooja knew she was losing Surya in one way. But by disagreeing with him and disallowing him, she would lose him in more than one way. She had decided to be the bigger person here and take whatever came her way with a pinch of salt. Her world and life were Ashna, and she knew that no one could take that away from her.

"Don't worry, Ashna will be fine. We have not left Ashna alone before this. I believe that's why you can't take your eyes off her. Relax. Pooja is a sweetheart, and Ashna is way more comfortable with Pooja than with me. So, they both will be fine." Saanvi consoled Surya.

The car left their residence area, and Saanvi wanted this precious alone time with Surya to not get wasted. This closeness and proximity with him is all that she had been waiting to have. She believed her accident had distanced them, and this trip would make things better for them. She held Surya's hand and rested her head on his shoulders. Surya took a deep breath, closed his eyes, and pretended to sleep during the journey. Saanvi kept smiling to herself. Her happiness had no bounds for finally getting what she was craving. These are special moments with Surya. She just wanted to be in his arms all her life. And it was going to be true in the next few hours.

Surya wanted to run away from everything, not only physically but mentally as well. He wanted to run away from his desires, his wishes, his love, his guilt, and this tearing pressure that was leading him towards the middle of nowhere.

They reached the hotel and checked into their room. It was a beautiful resort set up over the mountain overlooking the lake. The rooms were decorated with contemporary interiors, wooden floors, and wooden wall paneling.

Surya reached out for his phone placed next to Saanvi when Saanvi held his hand and requested, *"I ask for two days of you from you. Please, can I get them?"*

She hugged him tight and caressed his back. He slowly left and walked away. She went to him and enquired, *"Why this awkwardness? I am all yours. No distractions. No disturbance. No obstacles. No fears. No distances. No pressures. Haven't you waited for this time? Haven't you desired to be with me? It feels like you haven't touched me for years. To me, weeks are like years now. I love you and only you and will always love you until my last breath."*

He stood like a statue, like nothing had affected him. But he had a tear in the corner of his eye.

She was disheartened by his coldness and walked away. She sat on the seat overlooking the window, staring at the endless skies. She had tears in her eyes. She wondered what she had done wrong to not be loved back.

He walked out of the room and was about to lock it, and his heart started to race extremely fast. His legs weren't under his control. He rushed back in and went to Saanvi. He tapped her shoulder. She turned around and stood still as though she had given up all hope. He stared at her with tears in his eyes and a smile on his face. He hugged her tight. He hugged her so tight that there was no room for air to pass through between them. Both of them cried and kept weeping. They gradually felt each other's lips against each other, and they kissed.

The kiss was pure and long. Almost as if they were inseparable. This was that moment that had probably been playing in Saanvi's mind in the form of a dream for years now. She had just seen this moment and not been able to feel it until now.

With their arms around each other, they slowly moved toward the bed. Their tears couldn't stop. Slowly, they undressed each other and felt their souls uniting. Surya was lost in this magical moment. He was finally experiencing what he had stopped even desiring. He had trained his mind not to allow it to desire for this moment ever again. He was living it. There were no words being spoken, and probably, they weren't needed, either. They were **living the impossible dream**.

The two days that followed were a series of intimate moments. They didn't leave sight of each other. Surya was going to live his whole life in these couple of days. The punishment for one murder is death, and multiple murders is also death, is what he probably had running at the back of his mind while he was betraying Pooja innumerable times.

Their trip ended, and the moment of truth was getting closer for Surya as they were nearing to reach back home. Surya was into Saanvi, just like old times. He had no regret for the time he spent with Saanvi, but he sure was filled with immense guilt.

Saanvi had her arms around Surya's arms as they entered back home. Pooja's fear had turned true, she knew. She didn't have to ask Surya anything. His eyes conveyed it all. They were filled with content and guilt. His eyes were apologizing but neither sad nor angry.

Saanvi's overjoyed face proved that they had an amazing time with matters sorted between them. Nothing could turn back time or Pooja's decision. She was the third wheel in this trio now, is what she had sensed.

Surya and Pooja didn't speak to each other for the next couple of days. She wanted to leave, but that would mean the end of their relationship. She converted all her focus to her daughter Ashna.

Surya, on the other hand, couldn't meet her eye. He had wronged her faith in every way. He certainly did not want to leave Pooja, but now he did not want to leave Saanvi, too. He wanted to sail in two boats. He wanted to have the cake and eat it too.

10 SEPTEMBER 2016

CHAPTER 12

LIFE ALTERS

Surya got a call in the middle of the night. It was Sarita, Saanvi's mother.

"Surya, please bring Saanvi to the hospital urgently. It's very important."

"Aunty, what happened?"

"Ambar has gained consciousness."

Surya's eyes were damp. His throat was choked. Words failed to leave him.

He woke Saanvi and told her to get ready. He couldn't tell her anything more. Moreover, he didn't know what to say to her. He was so happy now with this situation, he didn't want to lose her.

Saanvi was anxious and kept nagging Surya with multiple questions. Surya had no idea how to revert.

They reached the hospital. Sarita Ji received them and took them to Ambar's room. Ambar looked at Saanvi. Saanvi looked at her Mom and asked her who Ambar was. Sarita Ji couldn't resist anymore and blurted out the truth, *"This is Ambar. You don't recognize him at all? He is your husband. He is the one with whom you have spent your last few years in Paris. Please try to remember."*

Saanvi started laughing blaringly. *"Surya, whose idea was this? Yours or Mom's? Nice prank, good effort, and a great idea. But I am not falling for it. It's funny. Hi, Ambar. Whose friend are you? You all are acting so well. Is the doctor aware that you all are using the hospital for all these games?"*

Sarita Ji lost control. She couldn't handle the situation anymore and felt embarrassed in front of Ambar. She slapped Saanvi across her face.

The room was filled with awkward silence. Saanvi fled out angrily. Surya ran behind her. She hugged him out in the corridor. Sarita Ji sat down nervously with her hands on her head.

Ambar watched all this drama unfold, clueless and in pain. He enquired, *"Aunty, what's going on? What just happened? Why did Saanvi behave like that?"*

"Son, unfortunately, when you met with an accident, you slipped into coma with your injuries, and Saanvi had some sort of memory loss. As per the doctors, she woke up in a virtual world. Probably, a dream in which she is stuck."

"What dream?"

"She believes she is married to her college friend, Surya, and they have a two-year-old daughter together."

Ambar was puzzled. His mind had given up on him. His world had been turned upside down with this news. He pulled himself together and asked for a practical solution.

"How long would it take for her to recover? Any treatment or procedure that can expedite the cure?"

"She has been like this ever since the accident. She gained consciousness and kept asking for Surya. We didn't understand. We showed her your condition, and she didn't recognize you at all. She has been living in Surya's house ever since, as recommended by the doctor. Any shock to her brain could do serious damage to her life. I was not supposed to tell her about you today. But I couldn't hold myself. I had a hope that she might gain her memory back if she saw you and spoke to you. But it was a vain exercise. I wish things could go back to how they were. Poor boy. Surya, his wife, and

daughter are all suffering because they are helping us." Sarita Ji explained the harsh reality.

Ambar was in too much pain to enquire any further and went back to sleep, hoping he was just seeing a nightmare.

Sarita Ji rushed out to follow Saanvi and Surya. They were in the waiting area of the hospital. Saanvi's tears kept rolling, and Surya was only patting his head. Sarita Ji looked at Surya, asking for permission to come to them. Surya closed his eyes and nodded to refuse.

Sarita Ji went to the doctor seeking future steps.

"Doctor, the situation has changed. You know that Ambar has gained consciousness. It has been too long; Saanvi hasn't stopped living her dream. It is high time she got back to actual reality. They have a life together, and Surya isn't part of it. And Surya has a life of his own, which is also getting affected. Please suggest some treatment which can normalize the current situation."

"Ma'am, I understand you. Please bring Saanvi to me. Let's conduct some tests to see her current situation."

Saanvi wasn't ready for any tests. She kept saying she was fine. She was getting out of control and burst into tears.

Surya held her cheeks in his hands and stared right into her eyes. *"Do you trust me?"*

She mellowed down. Her faith in him was infinite. She calmed down and permitted getting all tests and scans done.

Surya was not ready to let her go from his life. All his suppressed feelings had surfaced. He prayed for Saanvi's brain scans to have no improvement. He wished for her never to wake up from her dream.

WRONG

Duties or feelings
reality or dream
tough choices in life.
Why can't the heart and brain be a team?

Why do they always fight,
over things which are beyond?
Why don't they unite,
so I don't feel conned?

Why do I feel happy
burying off all the guilt?
I got what I had wanted.
Can't I keep both worlds that I have built?

Can't I go crazy
and have it all?
Why am I being told
now you have to take a call?

Do I have to choose to live
at a place where I don't belong?
Is being in love
and to be loved so wrong?

Test results were released. It was the moment of truth for Surya.

The doctor called Saanvi alone to his cabin and revealed to her that she was perfectly fine. Her previous cerebral activity had normalized. There seemed to be no abnormal activity anymore. *"Saanvi, your nerve damage has cleared up over time. You cannot be living in your dream now. You are pretending. You know the truth. You do recognize Ambar. You know Surya isn't your husband."*

"Yes, doctor, I know I can't fool you. It's true. You are right. A few days back, I woke up in a hotel, and I saw myself sleeping next to Surya and was astonished. I felt that I was dreaming once again. I kept lying down and staring at him asleep. He woke up and kissed my forehead. I was pleasantly stunned at that moment. He asked me if I was ok and if I was happy. He went overboard for me in that hotel room. I loved all the attention and all the special treatment from him. This is what I have always craved. I felt guilty but did not want to alter a moment of what was happening. I played along. Surya's wife also seemed to accept Surya's and my unity when we returned back to their home. I didn't want anyone to know the truth anymore. I know my cards are revealed. I have to go back to reality. My dream is over." Saanvi revealed with no choice.

The doctor asked Saanvi to tell everyone the truth. She requested the doctor not to reveal anything. She pleaded for some time.

"You are ruining a lot of lives, my dear. I can't play along with you in your lie. You are asking a lot from me."

"Doctor, I have finally reached a place in my life which I always wished for. My accident and my brain condition happened for a reason. I was meant to get back to Surya. He is the one I am supposed to be with. This is purely a heart issue. I know it's wrong, but I don't want to change a thing. Surya loves me back too. He wants to be with me too."

"No, he doesn't. He put up with all this charade only in humanity at my request. We were all trying to save you from death. That's it. Surya's wife sacrificed a lot just so that you could live. This is how you want to repay. And what about Ambar? I am no one to give you a moral lesson, but I think you are being extremely selfish, Saanvi. I will have to show your medical test results to your family and Surya. This is a hospital, and I am a doctor. I am not your friend who is going to support you in this. I apologize if my actions displease you, but I will have to do my job with honesty."

"Surya was pretending. He doesn't love me for real? Whatever it was, it meant the world to me. I wish I hadn't woken up from my dream ever."

"Well, you probably did wake up because you got what you had desired in the dream. It had been fulfilled. What did you do just before falling asleep that night?"

"I don't remember exactly. But from my next day's conversations with Surya and his actions towards me, I am guessing we had gotten intimate with each other."

"My best guess is that you lived your dream. It got fulfilled. So, it got over. Welcome back to reality. You should be happy you are not sick anymore. You can live a normal life. Make decisions for your life with complete consciousness, whatever they may be. "

"I don't have the guts to tell anyone that I have been pretending for the past few days."

The doctor felt for Saanvi. She was in tears.

"Well, the best way I can help you is not to reveal that your condition was ok for the past few days. I can hospitalize you, and we can pretend to begin a treatment and unfold the truth tomorrow, suggesting that the medication worked on you. This way, you won't be a liar, and everyone will ease into the process. Surya too would want to get back to his family."

"I am truly grateful, doctor."

The drama commenced. The doctor proceeded with hospitalization procedures for Saanvi. He informed Sarita Ji, Surya, and Ambar that he has seen some improvement in her scans and is hopeful that she may respond to a particular medication treatment he has in mind. Post, which he would be able to get back to them.

Sarita Ji and Ambar were thrilled to learn of this development for obvious reasons, but Surya turned cold. He wasn't excited that his life was going to go back to being normal with his wife and kid. Although he pretended to feel pleasant.

Surya returned home with mixed feelings. Pooja watched him enter alone without Saanvi and stared at him, hoping to get a reply. Their marriage was on the edge now, but she had hoped that things would go back to normal. Surya informed her gloomily, *"They have hospitalized her and put her on medication. Her scans have shown some improvement. She might get normal if the medicines work on her."*

This news was music to her ears, but Surya's expressions were the needles in her eyes. Saanvi's virtual world had ruined Pooja's real world. Her niceness had backstabbed her. She left everything on time now. It would either heal her or destroy her.

While Surya was melancholy, he also finally got some chance to play with his daughter. He distracted his mind from all this melodrama with his daughter's playfulness. She had started talking a little now and had lots to share with him about her and Pooja's exclusive time together. Pooja looked at them, and it brought some sense of relief in her mind. She thought to herself, and this scene reinforced her confidence - Surya may love Saanvi back, and he may fall out of love with Pooja, but he will never leave her as he is crazy about the apple of their eye, Aashna.

On the other hand, just when Saanvi had started making peace with her reality lying in the hospital bed, she closed her eyes. She could feel a sense of Surya's hands slipping away from her once again. She had been in these shoes years ago. She couldn't let it happen again. She had finally got Surya back in her life. Her obsession for Surya wasn't fading away yet. Was she ready to return to the life she had lived all these years? Was she ready to betray or separate from Ambar, who had held her hands always? The dilemma jolted her, and chills ran down her spine. What decision could she take? And what decision would Surya take if she decided to choose to be with Surya? Was Surya going to choose to live with her? Was he ready to leave his wife and daughter for her? Or was the doctor telling the truth about Surya only pretending all this while?

What if Surya didn't accept her? She did see love in his eyes for her. Or was it just concern out of humanity? No, it wasn't. She did feel his passion while they were intimate. Or were they mere moments of weakness?

Family vs love.

Saanvi had a long night to follow, with an overflow of questions and dilemmas. Her heart and mind were in a war zone with each other. Her personality had two sides talking to each other.

HUSBAND VS LOVE OF LIFE

Pros to choose Ambar

1. Ambar loves her, protects her, and takes care of her.
2. There is a ready settled life with a career and family.
3. Her parents and society will approve of her choice of Ambar.

Cons to choose Ambar

1. She will go back to living the same life with a lack of excitement.
2. She will never get to be with Surya again.
3. She would be answerable to Ambar about everything that happened with Surya while he was in coma and due to her medical condition.

4. Things may not remain the same between them after he found out about her desires.
5. She will return to being haunted by Surya in her dreams.
6. She may break Surya's heart again.

Pros to choose Surya

1. Surya is her love, her passion, her desire, her dream. This is what she really wants.
2. This was her only chance to get Surya back in her life.

Cons to choose Surya

1. Surya's family will break because of her.
2. Surya may not choose her back. In this case, she will neither be with Surya nor will she choose Ambar.
3. She will have to leave her settled life and career in Paris and move to a small city.
4. Ambar's heart will break.
5. Her parents' hearts will break.
6. It will be unfair to Pooja, who has been nothing but kind to her.

Harsh reality hit her. What she really wanted had only two positive factors. All the factors were against what she was desperately wishing to have as a future life. The list was clearly floating in front of her eyes. Her mind had triumphed over her heart and desires. Her wrong decision would destroy multiple bonds and relations and hurt innumerable sentiments. *'Since when did I become so selfish and insensitive?'* she questioned herself.

She hadn't slept all night pondering over all these thoughts. Sarita Ji, Ambar, Surya, Pooja, Ananya, and Karan entered her room at the wake of dawn. The moment of truth was about to be unveiled.

Saanvi slowly stood up and walked toward them. She walked past Surya and hugged Ambar tight.

She looked at them at the same time, puzzled. She pretended to not remember anything and asked, *"Hey guys, long time. So good to see you, too. What are you all doing here?"*

Surya stood still, frozen, chills ran through his spine. His mind had reached an epitome of taking these shocks from Saanvi. Pooja looked at Surya. His body wasn't moving. He wasn't crying, he wasn't smiling, and he wasn't changing his expression. He stood like an ice statue.

While Saanvi was talking to Ambar and Ananya, Pooja shook Surya to call him, and he collapsed. There was commotion in the hospital ward. Saanvi ran towards Surya, but Pooja pushed her away angrily. Saanvi couldn't hold her feelings and burst into tears and howled, "Surya, Surya, Surya!!!"

Surya was taken over by ward boys onto a stretcher to another ward. All of them followed the stretcher. The Doctor arrived and checked his pulse, blood pressure, and other vitals. All had dropped. He wasn't responding to anything. His eyes were open, but he could not respond.

Saanvi had ruined it all. Her one decision turned the lives of all once again. She began to cry incessantly. Ambar held Saanvi in a completely confused state of mind. Why is Saanvi behaving like Surya's wife? And why was Pooja not? Pooja's tears had dried. She knew all the truth, and the situation had detached her from Surya on some level. She wasn't feeling the pain that a wife should ideally feel. She was built with a larger ego now. She had sensed the fate of Surya. She had predicted Saanvi's betrayal in advance. She had hoped for Surya's heart not to be broken again but knew that it would eventually be. She kind of looked like she knew what was coming in store for Surya. Her emotions were controlled. Her expressions were those of being a responsible spouse and completing all the formalities of hospitalization.

Ambar couldn't resist asking at this stage. *"Saanvi, relax! Please stay calm. I know Surya was a very close friend of yours. But I am sure he will gain consciousness very soon. Don't worry! You seem to be crying a bit too much. Are you feeling guilty about not keeping in touch with him or something? As I don't understand the gravity of your sensitivity for an old college friend to this extent"*

She didn't have words to justify herself. She lacked the skills to continue pretending to be oblivious to her true feelings towards Surya. She broke down. Guilt encompassed her for Surya's current condition, and she blurted out the truth to Ambar. She dropped down on her knees and started rambling, *"I loved him, and I still do. He fainted because of me. Because I pretended not to care about him. I did this to him. Oh God, what did I do? Bring him back."* Her lips shivered and fingers trembled while words spluttered out of her.

"Calm down, Saanvi. Please get up. Hold your breath. I am all ears to you. Tell me what you want to say with clarity." Ambar showed support to her with immense patience.

"While you were in coma, I gained consciousness with a mental condition in which I was stuck in a dream. I had lost my present memory. I didn't remember you. I was married to my ex-lover, Surya, in my dream, and we had a happy life. I was stuck in my dream when I woke up after the accident and two weeks of coma. Doctors advised my mother and Surya that if they

didn't want to risk my life, they should all pretend that my dream was a reality. To help me not lose my life, Surya and his wife played along so that my condition wouldn't deteriorate. But during that time, Surya and I had our weak moments where love took over morality. We fell in love with each other all over again. We got intimate. His wife found out and distanced herself from him. I then woke up and remembered everything after a few weeks. But I loved what was happening. Living with Surya was what I had wanted all my life. And now I was finally getting it. So, I didn't reveal anything to anyone. Surya and I started living like a couple. A week later, we got a call from the hospital that you had gained consciousness. I saw you and realized what a mistake I had made. Circumstances brought me back to Surya. But now it was time to go back to you. So, this morning, I woke up and chose to pretend that I gained my memory back and do not remember anything about the life that I lived in a dream. I didn't have the courage to tell you any of this. So, I pretended not to remember any of this. But Surya was shocked by my behavior. He loves me, and I did this to him again. I betrayed him again. I can't see Surya like this. I am sorry, Ambar. I am so sorry. I can't tell you how sorry I am. My decisions have ruined multiple lives." Saanvi finally poured her heart and all the truth out. Years of emotions stuffed inside flew out in a matter of seconds.

It was very shocking for her to see Ambar's reaction after all this. She expected him to walk away or shout at her. But he did none of this. He held her and put her on a chair. He took her head on his lap and patted her head with love and care. He consoled her with his kindness and heart of gold. *"I always knew somewhere deep down that you were not all in on this marriage. You were making peace with what has come to you, but this isn't really what you wanted. You were happy but not satisfied. I suffocated myself all along as I was unaware of the solution that could bring a real smile to your face. I tried a lot for so many years, but I still didn't see you completely into me. My struggle is finally over. Today, I finally know why, and it has not angered me at all. Please don't apologize for loving someone. You deserve to be with the one you love. My love for you is one-sided and it will always be special for me. But you and Surya love each other. If his wife is able to happily accept this, then you must go ahead and spend your remaining life with him. I will always remain in your life as a well-wisher. Don't worry. Go to him. Take care of him. My blessings are with you. Once you are settled, I will free you legally as well. Right now, it's more important to take care of Surya. I will miss you, my baby. Take care of yourself, and I hope you can keep in touch and we remain friends."*

Saanvi and Ambar hugged each other. It was a goodbye Saanvi did not want to make. Both had tears in their eyes. She knew she had destroyed Ambar's life. And yet, Ambar didn't even complain. What was he made of? It would have been a lot easier to leave him if he had been mean to her about this. But it pained her a lot more than expected since he was so nice to her in spite of her betrayal.

Ambar knew forcing her to be with him would make no sense. He wasn't going to win her heart by doing so. Letting her go would have been the bigger thing to do. He was a nice guy. Ambar walked away. He went to Sarita Ji and touched her feet. He gave her a polite hug and whispered to her, *"I will always be your son. Please don't hesitate if you ever need anything. But please let Saanvi live with her love now. Don't stop them."* Ambar left out of the hospital.

Pooja witnessed all this drama unfold in front of her eyes. She watched Saanvi walk towards Surya's room. Saanvi was about to enter Surya's room when Pooja ran towards her.

"Stop, Saanvi. I have had enough of you. You misused my niceness a bit too much. I went above and beyond, trusting Surya. I know you both were in love, and that

is why, out of humanity, I tolerated everything. I kept quiet until now as I thought your life would be in danger if the truth was revealed. But here you were putting up an act after all. Such lies. Breaking my family. You do have a spine to stand in front of me. Your husband may be a sent angel for you. But he has nothing to lose. You were a lifeless wife for him anyway. I have everything to lose, Saanvi. My child can't be fatherless because of you. Surya and I had a very good life before you showed up at our doorstep one month ago. I won't let this month ruin my life and my family. I have had enough of all this drama. I will not allow you to come close to Surya anymore. He better believe that you forgot him due to the medicines last night. For God's sake and for the sake of our daughter, please leave and let us live like a family. If you have a little bit of humanity left, please just get lost."

Saanvi deserved this, after all. She was in the wrong in the eyes of Pooja. She stepped back. First her Mom and now Pooja. The universe would never let them come together. She didn't have the courage to fight once again. She wiped her tears, turned around, and walked away. Sarita Ji followed her and took her home.

SEPTEMBER TO DECEMBER 2016

CHAPTER 13

NEW MEANINGS

Saanvi didn't eat for a few days. This time, Sarita Ji didn't interfere with her life. She didn't have words to correct anything that had happened.

"Let's leave this town. Cursed town. Nothing positive came out of this place."

Saanvi was a moving dead body. She was doing as directed. She had no reason to live. They left town and moved back to her parents' city. She began to live a lifeless life.

One day, she was walking on the street and saw a group of small homeless kids walking on the rough road without any shoes. They came to her begging for money. She had seen it a trillion times earlier. But today was different. She was hollow from within. This was her moment to find meaning in her life. She decided to alter their lives in the best manner possible and not just by giving them money. She took those kids to an orphanage and requested the Manager to help her out for the welfare of these kids. She joined that charity as a volunteer. She helped the orphans. Smiles on their faces brought meaning to her so-called life she was living. A few days later, Ambar came to visit her. Sarita Ji had told him about her situation.

"I came here to ask you if you would like to come back with me. I am going back to Paris tomorrow. I know it doesn't make sense. But I think I should ask you."

"I have done so wrong with you. Yet, you continue being a gem. I can't keep ruining your life further. You don't deserve my betrayal, Ambar. I have nothing less than immense respect for you. You are a wonder and only deserve someone who loves you and gives you what you deserve. I am not capable of doing that. I hope you have a happy life with someone you find."

They bid goodbye to each other.

A couple of months later, he called her from Paris to inform her that she would receive divorce papers in the mail. If she had any concerns, she should call him without any hesitation. He also informed her that he had found someone whom he cares for and, once their divorce is complete, wishes to marry her.

She was happy in a way. At least one guilt off her chest.

She moved out of her parents' home and shifted to a ladies' PG with a few other working women. She started a small-time business with crafts made by the orphans. She would run it, and the funds she received, she used them for the welfare of the children. She grew the NGO and housed 25 children.

She decided never to look back to Ajmer again. She was never going to interfere in Surya and Pooja's family again.

She found a reason to live. She would spend all her time and energy on helping these children. Her life got a meaning, and she decided to make the most of the love she had inside her by sharing it with those who are loveless.

24 JUNE 2024

CHAPTER 14

THE CLOSURE

Eight years passed by. Saanvi had made a name for being a godmother in her city. She used a lot of funding from donors and built a chain of orphanage homes. She had about 1600 children under her shelter. The children whom she had sheltered and educated eight years ago had now found jobs in good companies. She was being interviewed for her NGO by a national television channel for her work. She was informed that they would go live with this interview.

Interviewer: *"What inspired you to help so many children?"*

Saanvi: *"Hi, dear. Thanks for taking the time to share my views and voice with a lot more people than I can manually access. To answer your question, I inspired myself. I did ruin a few lives, including my own, due to some wrong decisions. Had to reverse it by making some other lives better. I am not doing this for others. I am doing all of this for myself. I am trying to help myself. This is my therapy. One smile on someone's face I can bring makes me desire to live one more day. I am very selfish."*

Interviewer: *"That is very modest of you to say. You don't have a family of your own. You dedicated your entire life to them. It's not easy. You are mothering so many parentless children. You saved so many from turning into beggars. You shaped their lives. It's absolutely remarkable. You are anything but selfish. Anyway, please share your experience of how hard or easy it is to acquire funding in today's times."*

Saanvi: *"Virtuousness is all around us. There are innumerable souls blessed with substantial resources. We just need to reach out to them, and they will help spontaneously. With word of mouth, we have some donors reach out to us. So, it works out adequately."*

Interviewer: *"That is such an optimistic approach. Truly fabulous to see so much positivity. What is your vision for the future?"*

Saanvi: *"Honestly, I started off with no vision. My intention was to just keep helping each child that came my way. But reaching this stage, I now aim at having not a single uneducated child in this city. This city should become free of child beggars completely. I wish I could see every child that is under my shelter grow into fine human beings who not only do well for themselves but also continue this chain of helping out in their own way. That is my vision."*

Interviewer: *"Wow. That is truly a powerful vision. Any message for the audience?"*

Saanvi: *"I would like to encourage as many people as I can to help in whatever big or small way they can to aid my mission. I hope this interview can motivate a lot of people. Please connect with us to serve society a little. My contact details are given below."*

Interviewer: *"Yes, that was the aim of this interview. If anyone would like to help Saanvi Rawal in her mission to eradicate poverty and illiteracy from the city, please do connect with her directly on the mobile number shown on your TV screens below. Thank you, Saanvi, for your valuable time. Truly appreciate your intent, hard work and vision."*

Saanvi: *"In fact, I would like to thank you for helping me out to connect to a larger group of society."*

As soon as she removed her mike, she checked her phone. She had missed eight calls from an unknown number. She probably received calls from a generous donor, she hoped. She dialed back and heard an unexpected voice.

"Saanvi? It's Pooja here."

Saanvi could not believe her ears. She might be daydreaming. This was odd. Maybe someone else. She didn't reply anything and chose to stay quiet. Pooja continued to talk.

"Pooja, Surya's wife here."

"Hi, Pooja. Hope all is ok?"

"I have been trying to locate you for the past couple of months. But you are not available on any social media platforms. None of the friends knew your number. Finally watched your live interview on TV and saw your number. Called you immediately."

"Oh, I am sorry for this. After what happened earlier, I chose to disconnect myself completely. Is everything ok?"

"It's about Surya."

"What happened?"

"Can you come to Ajmer, please? I wouldn't bother you if it wasn't important. You know that."

"No, dear. I will never come back. I cannot. It took me years to find meaning in my life. And it took me years to convince myself to never bother your happy family again. I will not be the reason for your misery again."

"Saanvi, there is no happy family for you to ruin anymore. You already caused the damage years ago. It's

now time to mend your past. Please come. You are needed here."

"Huh?"

Saanvi froze over the phone. Her voice was stuck in her throat.

"Hello, are you there? Will you come, Saanvi?"

Hesitatingly, she agreed. *"Yes."*

Saanvi was so nervous to hear this news that her blood pressure dropped. She started perspiring immensely. Her fingers began to tremble. She sipped some water and gathered herself to book the first flight to Ajmer.

Saanvi packed her bags and reached the airport. She wasn't sure how she would react to this situation. Her heart was in her mouth at the thought of facing Surya again. What must have happened to him? Why was there no happy family left?

Saanvi reached the address Pooja gave her through the text message. She was welcomed by a cute young girl with a bright face and light brown eyes. She smiled and enquired, *"Are you Saanvi Aunty?"*

Saanvi nodded. *"Are you Aashna?"*

Aashna ran inside and called out to Pooja.

Pooja hugged Saanvi awkwardly and greeted her inside.

Pooja sat down and narrated her side of the past.

"So, after you left the hospital that day, I decided to never leave Surya's side. My anger was so peaked that I was all ready to blast him as soon as he'd gain consciousness. The doctors told me his blood pressure had dropped substantially. They moved him into the ICU within a few hours. That night was long. I waited for him to wake up. I cursed you for doing this to him. At the wake of dawn, the doctor arrived and woke me up with the news that Surya had slipped into a coma. I didn't know what to say."

Saanvi had tears in her eyes.

"Doctors said they expect him to get fine within a few weeks. I took care of him for weeks. But nothing. He was in the same vegetative state. Months passed, and then almost a year passed. My patience ended. I had to run my house, manage finances, and raise Aashna. I didn't have the liberty to break down. I told you I didn't want my daughter to be fatherless. Well, eventually, that's what was in store for her. I held myself together and started working. I took up a job and sent Aashna to daycare. I was making ends meet. Nights at the hospital and days running a single-woman show. I started

*spending a lot of time at the hospital. The hospital ward was my new home. Three years passed in this same situation, and there was not a single ray of hope left within me. The support and encouragement of the doctors kept me going. Surya's doctor, Dr. Vikram got very friendly with Aashna. He would get her presents and play with her. He would get his mother's cooked food and share it with me. I found comfort in him during that difficult time. He gave me the shoulder to cry on and, in my weak moments, an arm to hug. I wasn't angry with Surya anymore but had lots to say to him. I waited for years, and finally, six months ago, Surya gained consciousness. It was a miracle for us. He woke up, and his eyes looked around. I smiled at him. He smiled back. He looked tired and exhausted. His weak body shivered, and his breath was very slow. A tear rolled down his cheek. And he gasped, "**Saanvi?**" That moment, I finally broke down. My world shattered. I waited for eight years for this man and took care of him. He woke up and looked for you. I walked out of the room, took Aashna, and went away. I left him. He didn't deserve me. His parents took him home. He is alone now. Getting better slowly. I requested his parents to release me. We signed divorce papers. Last month, I got engaged to Doctor Vikram. After I had cooled down, I realized that both of you were not to be blamed. It was true love which had got separated, and it was my duty to get you both together. You are meant to* *be together, and I had to look for you. Ever since then, I have been trying to locate you. Finally, today I saw your interview."* Pooja was welling up while delivering her disastrous life in front of the only person she despised.

"Oh God. I am terribly sorry for everything. My thousand apologies wouldn't be enough for what I put you through. I can't undo anything."

"It's ok, Saanvi. You don't have to undo anything. We all have to accept our destiny. Certain things are just meant to be. Let's go to see Surya at his parent's house."

Pooja, Aashna, and Saanvi walked down to Surya's house. Pooja had rented an apartment close to Surya's parents' home to help them with whatever they needed and also so that Aashna could meet her father often. Aashna entered Surya's room, and he smiled and began to play with her. Saanvi stood by the door and knocked. Surya looked up and choked with tears. Saanvi dropped her bag and stared at him. Pooja looked at Aashna and gestured for her to come with her and walked away with Aashna. Surya couldn't believe his eyes. He had barely begun to start walking, so he couldn't move much. Looking at Saanvi, he dropped down on a chair next to him. It felt like a dream. Saanvi froze still at the door. There was no reaction from her side.

The moment was finally here for them to be together. And now there was no obstacle in their union, but it all was such a shock for them that they couldn't move. They kept staring at each other in awe. Was this real? After years of struggle and conflicts. No words, no tears, no gestures. It took time for them to process and comprehend this fact.

A journey that began at the age of 17 and took a pause at the age of 21 was finally reaching its destination when they turned 40. They kept staring at each other for an undefined time. Their entire life flashed before them. Every dream they had for each other. Every hope they had to be together. It was all encompassed in this one long moment of silence.

BREATHE

Fancying togetherness
is all we ask.
Reminiscing our past
our desires unmask.

Struggles and obstacles
is all we faced.
This love we had
was eternally to be chased.

Clasped in the moment
embracing the truth.
Years of being apart
destroying our youth.

Life finally has to offer
a second chance.
Capturing the whole life
within a glance.

Gratitude to destiny
for eventually making this real.
I finally ***breathe***
as it's no more surreal.

They will finally get to

Live

In a

Dream

Forever